THE UNEXPECTED GIFT

A novel of inspiration: A Marine reclaims purpose and trust through love and redemption

Dear Sharon - !
Best luck in pursuit of the arts,
PEO love,
Karen

Karen D. Nichols

Nichols' Books
In Black & White
Florence, OR

This is a work of fiction.

Nichols' Books – In Black & White
Florence, OR

Printed in the United States

Cover Design: Karen D. Nichols
Original photo of Heceta Beach
ISBN 13: 978-1481240291
ISBN 10: 1481240293
Website: www.florenceartists.com

ACKNOWLEDGEMENTS

Some very special people helped to bring this novel to fruition. Thank you: Coastal Writers for inspiration and helping me through the chapters, to Tom McCarville and Charles Walker in sharing their return from military life, to Staff Sergeant Michael Stout for information about military protocol, to Pastor Randy Paredes for his perspective on helping ex-military, to Pattie Brooks Anderson for help on the cover, for Him who seemed to put the information at my fingertips where I needed, when I needed it, to Him, without whose inspiration the novel would not have been completed, to my dog, Buddy, who gives no-strings-attached love and especially for my dear husband, who put up with my frustrations and shared my dream, for his invaluable input, editing and loving consideration of time to let me create. The final thank you goes to whoever invented the Internet where information is readily available.

For all those who have
been wounded and broken by tragedy
and dedicated to those who face
peril in the service of others

The Unexpected Gift

Karen Nichols

Chapter 1

Life is Change

Tragedy doesn't happen when one expects, and the shock of it can land like a boot to the gut, especially when it's a life-changing event. Though I should start where it all began.

My buddy Josh and I went way back. First came the games of catch with Josh's dad, who I adopted as my father figure when my dad passed away. Then there was little league. When we tried out for football in high school, we knew that was our sport. In varsity football, Josh had the arm and I had the legs. After graduation we went to the University of Oregon where Josh played quarterback and I played wide receiver.

Following a game five years ago, we discussed a terrorist attack we heard about in the news. We decided that we weren't going to be all talk. We went to Eugene, enlisted in the Marine Corps to report for duty after graduation.

The week after we graduated, I stood as best man at the wedding when Josh married his childhood sweetheart and my best friend, Juliana, or Jules, for short. The three of us had known each other since kindergarten.

I wish I had been there when Josh proposed. He brought her a dozen red roses. I can picture his silly grin as he came into her second grade classroom, got on one knee and said, "Juliana, will you marry me?" Apparently her second graders went wild cheering. Then they chanted, "Kiss her! Kiss Her!"

Weather cleared, making it a beautiful day to have the wedding on the beach. The sun sat low in the sky, sinking slowly into the ocean, with a backdrop of clouds and sun that only an Oregon sky can produce. Jules stepped past the fifty some guests, walking slowly to the rhythm as the soloist sang, "Ava Maria".

The sun glinted through the net of her veil, making her dark hair shimmer. A serene smile lit her face. I wondered if I had ever thought of Jules as beautiful before that moment. Josh wore an inane grin from dimple to dimple. He'd have probably laughed out loud had he seen himself standing there with the sun highlighting his blond hair like a halo.

The bride and groom wrote their own vows. How puzzling. Josh, of all people, repeated all that romantic stuff he wrote to her. It was as though there were only the two of them standing in the heavenly light of sunset. His sincerity never wavered even when the laughter started. The guests caught sight of the groom's shoe soles as they knelt before Pastor Perez. In white paint, his left shoe said, "He" and the right one said, "lp!" The audience covered their mouths, looked aside as they tried to stifle loud chortling, but an audible snickering spread like a cloud of laughing gas all during the vows.

I was glad. How would it look if the big Marine best man, Zackary Langston, stood there wiping his nose instead of smiling?

The reception was held upstairs at Driftwood shores overlooking the sea and the sands. Round tables draped in white linen with candles and white roses in the center were spread around where the wedding party sat at their head table.

Just after dinner, Josh fastened the watch around Jules' wrist.

I acted as his consultant when he picked out her wedding gift. That was the day we picked out the wedding suits. We doubled over in laughter when he stepped out of the dressing room in a baby blue tux with black piping. "Sixties here we come!"

"Tadah!" I danced out of the dressing room in tails and top hat doing my imitation of an old time tap dancer like in the movie, "The Artist". We thought it would be fun to wear tails over our Levi's, but Jules would kill us. In actuality, I did think the clerk would kill us before we picked out a nice conservative black tux. Our formal protest was to wear high top black tennis shoes.

That afternoon, Jules whispered to me, "Zack, do you think Josh would wear a St. Christopher's medal?"

The next day, I drove her to Skeie's Jewelers in Eugene. They only had one that she could afford so it was a quick decision. On our way back, because we had driven this 60 miles so often, we passed the time recounting happenings from our childhood. We laughed all the way as we remembered stuff.

Her sixth birthday party took place at Arby's Pizza. That'd teach her never to have boys at her party ever gain.

"Remember? A couple of guys started throwing sausage hunks at each other when one hit the waitress in the face," I said.

"That would have been just rude, if she hadn't been carrying my birthday cake."

"Until she tripped."

We chuckled.

"I can still see her dancing around and me, while I was struck silent thinking, "Please...Don't drop it!'" Jules said.

"I saw you scrunch your eyes shut when she got close and dropped the cake on the table right in front of you. Splat."

"Chunks of chocolate cake all over my brand new pink dress." She slid a strand of chestnut-colored hair behind her ear.

"Well, it didn't turn out so bad. Your mother managed to stick the candles in that mess and we did sing, 'Happy Birthday.'"

"I might have forgiven you guys if Josh hadn't yelled, "Dig

in!"

"Then all the guys dove in, grabbed handfuls of cake, stuffed it in their faces and licked their fingers like cave men. That was so cool."

Jules threw her fist into my shoulder.

"So that's why you didn't have a 'Bring-a-date' bridal shower," I said with mock surprise.

Rolling her eyes, she said. "I know you all too well."

She hugged herself and shivered. "Promise me. You guys will always, always watch out for each other and that you'll make sure he never takes this medal off." She squeezed my hand on the steering wheel. "I need the two of you back in one piece. Promise."

The trip home went silent. We mentioned a few more details about the wedding while we watched the rainfall splash across the windshield with the wipers chasing it around.

There were always little speeches expressing best wishes at weddings. Perspiration beaded on my forehead. I knew I was expected to say a few words to toast the bride and groom. Where does one start when you have a lifetime of experiences? Rising from my seat, I raised my champagne glass to give my well-practiced ode to my best friends.

"Okay Zack, you promised." Jules whispered.

I knew she thought that I'd pull some joke or relate some embarrassing moment. Of course, she wouldn't have been wrong.

To the contrary, my throat felt strangled. I reached up to loosen my collar and tie. "To my best friends, forever," is the extent of what I managed to croak out. I downed the champagne while the other hand crumpled the sentimental essay including the red-faced events, I had penned but stuffed into my pocket.

The last golden glow over the ocean shone through the windows while Josh and Jules held each other close in their first dance as Mr. and Mrs. Joshua Cole.

A nostalgic scene flashed before my eyes. Like a movie I saw the three of us tumbling over, climbing in and out of the jungle gym at the elementary school playground, surrounded in the laughter of our friendship. I stood for a while to let that moment replay. Who'd have thought then that the two of them would be married one day with the two of us heading to Marine boot camp?

The cake scene came next. They promised each other they wouldn't smash the cake pieces into each other's faces. So neatly, Josh popped a piece into Jules' open mouth as she did the same to him. He then grabbed her in a monster hug and kissed her. That had a similar affect though, as a smash, with the chocolate crumbs and white frosting decorating their faces.

Knowing their penchant for retro Elvis music, I sauntered over to the DJ and asked him to play, "You Ain't Nothing But a Hound Dog", an appropriate title for the guy that beat me to the altar. With the music blaring and the beat resonating, I grabbed Jules for the last crazy dance I'd get with her for a long while. I whipped into my 'Dance With the Stars' mode, picked her up, swung her around doing a few flips and twirl moves before I returned her to Josh.

Encircled by the guests, Jules sat in the satin-lined chair, lifted a handful of white fluffy dress hem to a modest level, while Josh stuck his head under. A "Whoa" went up from the crowd. He slid the baby blue garter down her long leg. All the single guys were goaded into standing around waiting for Josh to fling it. The garter flew from Josh's hand sailing over the throng of guys right into mine, like I'd caught so many of his passes on the football field. I gazed at it for a second and thrust my arm in the air while I spun it around like a lasso over my head.

Kylie, in a blue silk dress clinging to her ever so lovely derriere, sidled up to me. "Dance with me, Zack."

The band played a slow song, so I pressed her close and rocked to the music. Unfortunately for me, she had a lot going for her, with her own following of guys who wanted to dance with her. I guessed that I wasn't going to get lucky with her tonight.

So then I had to spend the rest of the evening drinking too much, gyrating and otherwise being obnoxious so I wouldn't be chased by a couple of marriageables, especially my old girlfriend, who kept asking me to dance.

By the time the reception waned, Josh and Jules forgave me for the message on the bottom of Josh's shoes.

The bride and groom rushed off to change their clothes. Josh came ambling back in his jeans and sweatshirt.

With two shots of Jack Daniels, I joined him at the window overlooking the shore.

"She'll take forever," Josh checked his watch. "Let's time it."

"Yeah, I remember when we doubled for the prom, while my date and I had to wait in the limo for a half an hour while Jules finished her makeup." I scratched my head.

"And your date was Annie, the minister's daughter."

"She was … well…nice."

"Yeah." He stared out to sea for a moment. "Ever think we would be joining the Marines?"

"You remember the base camp we set up in your back yard? We brandished our arsenal of dart guns, dashing around the neighborhood, hiding behind bushes, blasting imaginary shots and lobbing grenades."

"We stacked all those sticks together for a fort only to have it cave in on us when we caught the enemy sneaking up on us," Josh said.

We Laughed.

"The Morrison brothers. Wonder what ever happened to them."

Josh wiped his forehead. "I almost forgot that army phase we went through."

"Well, here's to our new phase! Skoal!"

Down went the Jack in a synchronized gulp.

Josh checked his watch. "Twenty-five minutes."

Jules sauntered up, her fancy hairdo swept away into a

swaying ponytail.

"Hey, you beat your record." I kissed Jules.

Josh took her bags out to the car and stowed them in his trunk sauntering back in with his hands in his pockets ~~on her chee~~k.

Hugging and laughing, the newlyweds headed downstairs toward the exit.

After the parents said their goodbyes, I moved in. I allotted the bear bug to Josh then swung Jules in the air.

"Call me as soon as you get there!" I laughed.

"Yeah, right!"

They ducked, scampered for the car, as the guests showered rice all over them. I visualized the seagulls swooping in plucking up all that rice when the people drove away leaving the parking lot an open feast for them.

When Mr. and Mrs. Joshua Cole drove off in the moonlight, the cans clanging behind the car, I wiped my nose. Was I envious that I had not found my 'one and only' or nostalgic that nothing would ever be the same again? I know I never felt luckier in my life knowing the two of them would always be my best friends.

I didn't know then. Nothing lasts forever.

Chapter 2

Getting Ready to Get Ready

I knew that the expectations for Marine Corps Basic training were the most stringent of all the services. Even though we'd worked out with the team during football season, which was several months back, Josh and I had to get ourselves back in shape. A web check gave me regulation military exercises and stretches to do. So before the wedding, I drove my Jeep Wrangler to Miller Park a couple of days to meet Josh. My German Shepherd, Beast, came with me everywhere I could take him, however dogs were not allowed at the park, so we switched to the high school track, fitting in when no one was using the facility.

Jules came out on weekends as our coach. "Down and give me a hundred." she yelled. When we finished, she'd yell, "50 more! This time do 'em right!" We did our version of a triathlon: 150 push-ups, 100 pull-ups, 100 sit-ups then a run a couple of miles around the track. We did 30-second sprints, 60-second walks and some jogging. After lunch, we'd do it all again. Beast was a great help in training, racing around the track with us. He was so smart. He got the idea it was a race. I couldn't believe how fast he was for an eleven year-old dog. We'd try to catch him. There he'd be, sitting by Jules when we came back around to her. Though sometimes Beast would be yapping at our heels, barking like, "Faster, guys."

Jules' favorite pushups were the pyramid where we'd be on ground level before she climbed on our backs. The three of us did those pushups until my arms quivered like jelly.

Sprinting around the track, Jules would heckle us, "Come on! You can go faster than that!" With her hand cupped around her mouth, she hollered, "Now you're running like girls! Pick it up!"

Josh goaded back. "Yeah! Why don't you come out and demonstrate, so we know how not to run?"

"Yeah!" she raced onto the field. When she caught up, we zoomed ahead. Sometimes we'd run ahead of her, then go nuts running backwards, so she could catch up. Once we all ran into each other, the three of us landing on our butts, rolling around in the dirt, laughing like crazy, with Beast licking our faces.

"Jules, time us."

We hunched into racing position.

"Ready set go!"

I'd let Josh dart ahead of me then I'd turbo-charge just barely in front. I was always the victor, but sometimes I'd hold back and let him win by a nose.

I had never been one to shinny up a pole, much less a rope, so we strung a couple of ropes on a cedar tree out back of Josh's place. At first we'd fall off about half way up. However, soon we were racing each other to the top. Jules had her stopwatch out everyday after she came home from her teaching job and on weekends. Josh could always beat me up that dang rope. So one day I greased his rope with Wesson oil making that time the only time I won.

Beast tried his version by grasping the rope in his teeth, gyrating, which resulted in spinning himself around. When he finally dropped off, he reeled around like we'd fed him beer, providing a good laugh for us.

Jules tried the rope a few times and finally made it up one afternoon. She slapped my raised palm "That's it for me," she said, dusting off her sore hands with a handful of dirt.

My calluses began to build up after the blisters popped. When we finally left for basic training, my hands were tough.

Shortly after their honeymoon at the Adobe Inn in Yachats,

both our orders came giving us seven days to report to Camp Pendleton in Southern California. That meant we'd only have a few more days to train. We intensified.

I'd fall into bed each night at 8 PM set the alarm to ring at 4AM, followed by instant slumber. I wondered how Josh did it with all the alone time he and Jules carved out of their schedules. Maybe I just wished I had someone to fall into bed with.

The night before I had to catch my airplane, I began to separate the bare essentials I needed to take to basic training. If I weren't such a last-minute person, it'd be done.

After training one day, Josh warned me. "Zack, when are you gonna get it together? I've got most of my stuff ready to load into my duffle bag. So you haven't even begun, I bet."

"Yeah, yeah, I'll do it tonight." Yeah, Yeah, why didn't I do it?

With the usual wind and rain, I wakened from a toss-and-turn night I spent, both in nightmares of the rigors some sergeant putting me through in basic training, churning with apprehension for what's to follow. The plane for San Diego was leaving at 7:40 AM from Eugene, so I rushed around at 4 AM stowing the last of my gear.

The waffles were warming in the oven wafting an aroma that drew me into the kitchen. What a trooper. Mom got up to make me my favorite breakfast, her hair still pinned up in those dumb rollers. While she cracked the eggs into the skillet and crumbled the sausage in, I glanced around at the kitchen noticing the checkered curtains at the window. Why had I barely noticed them before? I paused to take a last look through that window. It would be a long time before I saw the forested backyard again, or for that matter, any part of the small cottage where we lived.

I scraped the last of the eggs and syrup off my plate then put my dishes on the counter. Nothing would taste this good for a long time.

"Come on, Mom, don't do that."

Mom reached up and wiped her nose with a paper towel. She

wrapped her arms around my neck and hugged me.

"I just don't know what I'm going to do without you around."

"Beast'll keep you company." I scratched behind his ears.

"Yeah but..." She sniffed.

"Aw Mom, you're going to be just fine. Maybe you'll go do some of that art thing you used to do."

"I could take some classes at LCC. Lane County Community College is always sending out those fliers."

"Or maybe you won't have time, because you'll meet some guy and take a cruise around the world."

"Sure like they're lined up out on the sidewalk waiting to ask."

"Well, just don't wear those dumb curlers when you find Mr. Right."

I escaped back to my room with Beast right behind me. He leaped on me, knocking me flat on the bed. Pinning me, he licked his warm tongue over my face then rolled on his back, my cue to wrestle with him. I checked the time as I jostled him around. "Enough Beast!" Docilely, he rolled over exposing his stomach for his usual rub down. He looked up at me with his sad watery eyes, reminding me how hard this goodbye was going to be.

Chapter 3

Of Days Gone By

I scanned my room, wiping my eyes. The dark blue walls were still covered with my posters from high school. I suddenly plunged into a flood of memories. Over my bed were the pennants from the U of O, along with the shelf of trophies from swimming, track and football. Pictures of my little league team, the Yankees, and more trophies were lined up against one wall.

On the dresser stood the picture of Josh and me, arms around each other's neck, horse grins spread across our faces. "Ah…2000… the turn of the century. The Yankees were 10 and 1." The flashback of that championship game came roaring through my mind like a stadium full of our cheering fans.

Jules cheered on the sidelines with her friend Kylie, dressed in green and gold outfits they had sewn up so they could be our official cheerleaders.

It was the bottom of the fifth. Josh approached the batter's box. Jules had the fans up on their feet. "Homer! Homer! Homer!" the crowd chanted. Josh whacked one out to left field. Two runs sped across home plate, the last one narrowly missing the catcher's tag as he slid past. Not a homer, but those runs tied the game. Josh was stuck in a pickle running back and forth between first and second base until the second baseman lunged tagging him out.

During the top of the sixth, the Red Sox scored three more times. With the Yankees now down those three runs, Billy stepped up to the plate. He spun around past three pitches without touching the ball. One down, Ken walked to the plate, bat on his shoulder, adjusting his batting helmet. A collective gasp went up each time a huge hit fell in foul territory, some 10 times. When he finally belted a high fly, it plunked snuggly into right fielder's glove. We all shuddered. Two out, no one on. Was it all over?

Joe swaggered up, butt out, swaying his bat back and forth. The pitcher lobbed one, high and outside. Joe swung. The ball smashed the pitcher in the shoulder. While he struggled to control the ball, Joe's foot hit the bag before the ball smacked into the first baseman's mitt. Next, Keith marched out stepping into the batter's box. The first pitch hit him in the hip. He danced around for a minute then limped to first as Joe jogged on to second. Our best hitter, Charles, strode up to the plate like he owned it. He swung, slashing through the air. The second pitch flew past him.

"Stee-rike two."

The crowd gasped.

With the third pitch, he hit a line drive. The First baseman dove for it and missed. By the time he'd recovered the ball and shot it to the second baseman, the bases were loaded,

I had been warming up on deck. I swallowed the lump in my throat and walked to the plate. Now there were two outs, the bases were loaded, in the bottom of the sixth.

I barely heard Jules yelling, "You can do it Zack. Knock it outta here!"

A perfect pitch whizzed past me. "Stee-rike one," the umpire held up his arm. The next pitch slid in way low and inside. I wiped my forehead with the back of my hand while my heart hammered in my chest. "One and One," the ump yelled. I couldn't believe the next pitch fired in a little on the low side, my favorite pitch. I killed it, but it landed foul. Sweat dripped like it was 90 degrees out, a temp not likely in Oregon, even in June. The pitch came. Without even thinking, I swung easy, straight on through. You know how you can feel it when you connect just right? When you hit that sweet spot? After the crack of the bat, I stood keeping my eye on the ball as it sailed over the left fielder's outstretched glove. It continued over the fence. I jogged around the bases waving my cap to the fans.

Jules jumped up and down on the sidelines screaming and waving those pompoms. The team rushed out, picked me up and carried me off the field. We won by one run, my grand slam deciding the championship.

Josh locked Jules in a hug, hopping up and down. Kylie jumped up, clasped her arms around my neck and gave me my first real kiss on the lips, and I thought that was the best day of my life. Boy was I wrong.

I smiled, remembering how I loved a little hero worship.

The horn sounded outside bringing an end to my life as I knew it.

Chapter 4

San Diego Here We Come

Josh's dad came by to pick me up for the airport. The Mustang sat idling by the curb. Dragging myself through the hall away from my room, Beast and I headed to the font door.

Kneeling, I nuzzled my face in his fur. "No, Beast." I wrapped my arms around him. "You can't go with us this time."

With the rain beating down, I kissed my mom.

She clung hard to me. Then she leaned back and drilled her stare intently into my eyes. She patted my cheek. "Go on, now. Don't you dare get into any trouble, you hear me, Zachary Langston."

I raced out to curb between raindrops where the shiny black '67 Mustang waited to take Josh and me to the Airport in Eugene. I lobbed my duffle bag in the trunk. Staring back at Mom silhouetted in the doorway, holding Beast by the collar, I suddenly realized how final that moment was.

With a quick salute, I hopped in the car. We were off. The whimpering of my dog in the distance mercifully tapered away.
Josh and Jules were in the back seat, so I jumped in front with Josh's dad, Donald Cole, who always insisted I address him as Don. A couple of times he caught me calling him 'Pop'. Not surprising. Since I was 10, he had treated me like his second son.

"I never thought we'd get this old Mustang on the road," I said as I shut the door.

Don had included me with Josh on Saturdays when they

worked on the Mustang. Jules kept hanging around even when Josh hung a sign on the garage that said, "No Girls allowed."

"Yeah, Dad." Josh leaned forward. "Remember on my tenth birthday, when you dragged that carcass of a wreck up the driveway? The rag top caved in on top of the seats all ripped up with the stuffing hanging out."

I scratched my head. "Your mom stood there with her hands on hips yelling, 'You take that back to what ever dump it came from…' She must have seen your pop's face because she relented, 'or at least build a garage for it.' And we did."

"Kelly never did get used to us working on this baby." Don tapped the dashboard letting out a loud chuckle. "You should have seen the look on your face when I told you it was your birthday present. You ran inside so fast I didn't have time to tell you it would be for your sixteenth birthday."

Jules turned toward Josh, "We were all up in your room trying to cheer you up when you kicked the door shut and locked yourself in the bathroom. When we finally coaxed you out, your eyes were all red. You were completely oblivious to the fact that your real birthday present, a ten speed, sat in the hallway."

I turned around. "I told you I'd take the bike if you didn't want it. That brought you out of your funk."

"Yeah, Dad, then every birthday or Christmas thereafter, you'd tell me that the transmission, or the drive shaft you just brought home was my present. By the time the tires and the mag rims came…now those actually did feel like gifts."

"I don't know how you got anything done with all the 'help'." Jules held up her fingers in quote signs. "I still have a copy of the picture that Kelly took with five sets of legs sticking out from under the car counting Beast who lay flat out, nose under, watching us."

"Thanks, Don, for letting me in on the last surprise when Josh's sixteenth birthday finally rolled around…" I said. "The Black Thunder sitting with its shiny new paint job and new rag top just sitting in my garage, until the big day."

"I'm going to miss her while I'm gone." Josh gave the seat a pat.

"Don't worry, I'll take good care of her." Jules grinned while she rubbed her hands together, grinning ear to ear.

"I told Dad to take it back if you don't behave yourself." Josh pointed a finger at her.

"I'm so proud of you guys," Don said.

Silence settled in like an intruder blocking out that childish part of our lives, reminding us all where Josh and I were headed. This could be a one-way trip. It felt like someone was sitting on my chest.

Josh sat cuddled up with Jules whispering in the backseat, while Don and I watched the wiper blades chase each other back and forth across the windshield. As we passed each landmark along Highway 126, I memorized the details. Some time in the near future I might want to recall this picture.

At the airport, check in went quickly since our plane sat on the runway to be the first to take off that morning.

I never realized how hard all these goodbyes would be. Don shook my hand. I hooked my arm around for a quick hug.

I checked out Josh's face, a mirror of my mine. Don embraced Josh in a big old bear hug. His shoulders were shaking as he turned sulking away, "I'll be over there, guys."

I wiped the back of my hand across my eyes.

Jules wasn't very happy about sending us both off to Afghanistan, which was sure to be our destination, but her patriotism was as strong as ours. Though she smiled, I knew she'd break down as soon as we disappeared out of sight.

Locked in a hug Jules kissed me on the cheek. She turned to Josh, her eyes brimming. She reached up, lifted his St. Christopher's medal from inside the neckline of his shirt and kissed it. When she started to sniffle, I left them alone for their final goodbyes. I walked up the ramp giving them all a goodbye salute.

Josh had been able to spend a weekend with Jules before we left. It was easier for me, because I broke up with my girl friend months before our decision to join the corps.

He plunked down next to me on the plane. "Semper Fi." We slapped palms.

To Portland, the small cigar shaped plane was less than an hour's ride, gratefully so. I was about to stuff a napkin down the screaming kid's throat. After a couple hours layover, we transferred onto a Delta flight for our trip to San Diego. Yeah! No kids on that flight!

I spent a lot of time walking the aisle after the beverage cart finished its run. I made the excuse to the flight attendant, "Just exercising." I didn't want to admit to even Josh that I was jumping out of my skin.

The flight attendant flipped her blonde braid over her shoulder. When she winked an alluring green eye as she walked by me, that was all I needed to corner her for a bit of mindless chatter in the galley, thus taking me out of my apprehensive mood for a while before she resumed her duties. Probably ten years older than me, she didn't mind talking to me. I found myself wishing I could take her out when we landed, if I didn't have a more important date.

After deplaning, we walked down the ramp, feeling a bit empty, watching others hugging and smiling at their greeters with no one there to greet us.

Then we caught the bus to the Recruit Depot. The trip was nearly over, but now I was Marine. And that would be another trip.

Chapter 5

In Training

Marine Corps Recruit Depot at San Diego: The first thing off the bus we absorbed the positive effect of sunshine in San Diego's warm weather. We had just come from Oregon where we thought getting warm happened when the thermometer hit 70 degrees. Though it was only 85 degrees, we were hot.

The training program proved more challenging that I had ever imagined. I am not sure how bad it would have been if we hadn't trained before we left. We were in better shape than half the guys, but that didn't help much. Some of them were a lot younger, though I doubt that helped them much either.

One of the first experiences came the chance to see what I would look like bald. In a matter of minutes, the 'hairdresser' buzzed off my spikey dark hair into my first regulation haircut. Then I lined up to get the physical. Being different sizes, didn't change the fact that we all looked like brothers lined up in our white skivvies.

The Drill Sergeant Hodges let us know early on. "Your mental and physical training is designed to put you in the best shape you will every be, thus create an instant willingness to obey any order given. Any order! Is that clear?"

"Yes Sir!" came the group response as we all lined up in our fatigues. By then I wondered if our own mothers could tell us apart.

Any reluctance, body language or smirk Sarge perceived on our part earned a regimen of push-ups, a trudging back and forth in the rain carrying our M16 assault rifles overhead, exhausting marches or watch out if you were in martial arts training that day.

I'm sure he perceived his professional duty to act as the chief tormentor while he carried out his relentless intimidation. The worst task occurred when we were sent out to 'smokers field', stripping cigarette buts, an endless chore. And If I ever hear, "I don't know what you've been told..."chanted again... Never got used to the 0300-hour wake up calls with Sergeant Hodges screaming in my face.

Recruit training was divided into three phases. Phase I instilled basic learning; physical and mental. Here I was to be stripped of my civilian life to be rebuilt into a Marine. Phase II weapons training including rifle practice. Phase III inflicted endurance training which encompassed what is dubbed, "The Longest Day," an 18-hour endurance test – 2,000-yard swim, wearing an 80-pound pack with distance running, rowing and swimming while carrying a watercraft.

After a few weeks of instruction on military history, Marine customs, basic first aid, we qualified in levels of swim/water survival to increase our survivability in an amphibious environment. Though once on a swim team, an area where I excelled, this turned out to be a grueling training program.

What a trip, the first time I hung down suspended, it seemed, thousands of feet in the air, while rappelling the tower.

Grunt life varied from day to day. Monday we were trucked, marched, or heloed if we were lucky, into the field, for three or four days, of land navigation and live ammo training. By the time were through I had a real intimate relationship with mud pits I either fell into or crawled on my belly through. Something to remember, California clay has a distinctive taste of which I became quite intimate.

Reveille roused us at 0530 with chow at 0615 then Formations at 0730. We trained in drills. Hours were spent cleaning, especially on Fridays. The Marine Corps provided us an endless supply of, gear, latrines and weapons that needed to be scoured.

Sometime we raced. "Ready, set, go!" We'd grab our

M16A2 assault rifles, disassemble, clean and reassemble them at record speeds. I had it down pat so I won eight times out of ten. Then the guys thought they'd fool me. They snapped the lights out. I could do it in the dark just as fast.

Josh earned his ranking as the platoon's top marksman. Out on Charlie Range we lined up for rifle and pistol training with moving target exercise. Josh took aim and blasted through them all without a miss. That earned him the Leatherneck Award - Perfect score on the Rifle Range.

There were classes on chemical warfare, inserting and extracting from helicopters – what a rush.

Every week a duty platoon did all work parties, cleaning company offices, supply areas, motor-t to clean the Humvees. The Marine Corps had a more rigorous educational program than the other services. Somehow, classes, martial arts and weapons training fit into our schedule.

Since I had outside experience with dog training, I spent time working with the canine unit. Beside target practice, I'd rank that as my favorite part of basic training.

We all wondered about how real live ammo practice was conducted. When we spent two days in the field with the live fire exercises, I got to find out. No one got shot during training. Though I wondered why not as we dropped below the 18-inch high barbed wire, stretched flat on our bellies, weapons extended out in front, crawling and turning over as the ammo zipped inches above our heads. One never forgets that whizzing sound of live ammo skimming along side of your head.

It wouldn't be long. We would find out how real combat was.

Chapter 6

Camp Leatherneck

An eight and a half month tour at Camp Leatherneck, Afghanistan spread ahead of us like an eternity, yet surprising the months ticked off rapidly.

I thought the heat was bad in California in July. Boy was I wrong. Deplaning, we were hit in the face with a dry gust of wind packing the punch of a blowtorch filled with sand, burning at a mild 110 degrees. Afghanistan welcomed us. As I surveyed the horizon, the scene seemed like a still photo shot through a brown tinted lens, flat sand, for as far as I could see.

A bus picked us up to take us to the massive barracks complex. On the way, the sergeant gave us a running commentary like we were on a vacation tour bus. "Welcome to Marine-istan... Camp Leatherneck...Ah, desert, a luscious brown, uninterrupted as far as the eye can see, here in the Palm Springs of Helmand. The Golf tournament is temporarily suspended due to frequent sandstorms. Here, the Nordstrom's' PX offers the finest shopping for hundreds of miles. We are now approaching the "Helmand Hilton" your home away from home. Your accommodations are warm and inviting with plenty of companionship..."

The rows of tents, half-mooned shaped like Quonset huts spread out ahead of us.

He pointed to the row of outhouses, with a line of soldiers waiting. "This is the Jarhead dance line...yonder, this fine dining establishment, commonly referred to as the mess hall, offers an 'interesting" menu...' He held up his fingers in quotation marks,

"And waiting for you is the excellent cuisine, with all the atmosphere one would expect for an establishment such as this."

The only spot of green clinging to the desert sand was a garden patch where a bit of farming made fresh vegetables appear in our "fine dining establishment", or perhaps the occasional poppy fields we were sent to destroy.

Afghani sand has a distinctive taste and texture. It permeated our barracks, our clothes, and our body orifices, with a vengeance.

It didn't take long to miss the majestic green forests of home, the vast expanse of ocean topped by the azure sky filled with billowing clouds that characterize Oregon. The rain we complained about so constantly seemed quite wonderful in my distant memory.

Maybe it's easier to write an account, because no one asks questions. Sometime the nightmares come. However, I've also found that writing the facts down acts like a hurdle. I feel anxiety as I approach my hurdle, but then I feel much calmer after I'm over it.

I thank God when I think how lucky I was that Josh was always at my side, though I often called him Cole while in the company of other military personnel. On Helmand base near Kandahar above Camp Leatherneck, having my buddy, at my back on those 21 missions, secured our friendship like bonds of steel.

My father never did talk about his time in the war zone. Now I understand. It's difficult to talk about my Afghan tour. Being at the front of the Taliban insurgency, the memories are so vividly horrendous. I made up my mind that I would make myself write, so I began to keep a journal. I did so for me, for me to weed out my demons. Perhaps few will ever read my ramblings, however, these writings helped me through.

One experience left an enduring mark on my soul.

The market place had a reputation as quite a dangerous place, proving to be the Taliban's favorite locale to make its terrorist statement. The large open area offered space for vendors to spread out their wares. A few shoppers moved from one vendor to the next, picking up cloth, vegetables or utensils to examine them for purchase. Mothers kept their small children close. However, several older children ran about giggling while chasing each other in the open areas.

It was a regular spot for our patrol to cover. The five Afghan National Army forces spread out. Cole went over to examine some cloth at a vendor's stall. There had not been an incident for a couple of months. Perhaps we were complacent. Matthew, Matt Hayworth, our youngest team member smiled at some kids, reached down from his lanky six-foot stance and handed them some candy. Santos and I were joking with each other, still surveying the rooftops, windows or alleyways. That's when I saw the robed woman in the window, her face contorted in a mask of fear, her brow furrowed with her mouth open in a silent scream. I followed her line of vision.

A lone man walked slowly to the center of the marketplace. His face twisted, as though he were in terrible pain. I walked toward him when he began speaking in spurts.

I signaled, "Hey, Haseeb." Our interpreter, a slight wiry Afghan soldier trotted over. That's when I saw the belt strapped to man's midriff.

"IED!" I raised my weapon. "Halt!"

Haseeb rapidly interpreted, "He's asking for help. He is not participating voluntarily. He's begging for help. He says he's a father. He doesn't want to die."

I couldn't tell if it was sweat or tears, rolling down the victim's face. He raised his hands. Parts of the IED sparkled in the intense sun, as his loose overcoat parted in the breeze.

"Clear the area!" Santos, the resident bomb expert, yelled. He jogged over to where the Afghan man stood trembling.

The Afghan soldiers rushed around the square grabbing up the children and herding the shoppers to safety.

I glanced around checking for weapons aimed in our direction. On the second floor, the woman held the child tight to her side and wrapped her burka around him. In a greatly pained grimace she stared wide-eyed at the man below her. She yelled down. The man raised his hand gesturing for her to get back.

"Roof line, clear!" I yelled, still sweeping my eyes around for anyone with a cell phone that might activate the bomb, my rifle at the ready.

Santos approached the device. For a man, husky as a side of beef, his fingers were long and slender. "It's on a timer." Santos examined it. "We have about six minutes..."

He helped the man out of his coat. Horror distorted the man's face while his body trembled. Santos tracked the wires woven around the man's waist and over his shoulders, like a suit of chain mail.

Haseeb asked his name.

"Afsoon," he managed to croak out.

"Tell him I will try to remove it, but I can't disarm this in time."

The man responded with an anguished, "Ahhh."

Santos began clipping the wires, one at a time.

The clock continued its insidious ticking. I wiped my forehead and the back of my neck. The red numbers flicked by while I stood watch.

With four minutes left, there still seemed like there were hundreds of wires yet to clip while the minutes ticked away. Santos continued slicing through the mail. He hit one wire that set off a loud buzz. The timer's red numbers flipped downward on super speed.

"I'm sorry, Afsoon."

Santos dragged me away stumbling before we sped off in an all out dash toward the Humvee.

I jammed my hands in my ears as Afsoon's scream dissolved into the blast of the explosion.

In those brief six minutes, I bonded so close with this anguished soul, so close, I felt as though I had lost a buddy. It would be years before I lost the image of his face and that of his wife helplessly watching her husband die. Through this incident including many others, we were reminded that we were here trying to put an end to the people living in this deadly fear.

Arriving at the Humvee, I shook all over as I clamped my hands over my ears to stop the gongs going off.

I couldn't hear, but it was obvious from the exaggerated gestures that Josh was screaming, "Hey, Old Buddy." Josh slugged my shoulder as I stepped into the Humvee. "How come you didn't run that fast when I'd throw you one in the end zone?" He gave me a quick shoulder and followed it with a jab. "Never so glad to see your ugly face coming through that blast."

After watching him mouth the words, I shook my head and gestured toward my ringing ears. I slung my arm around Josh's shoulder. "Kinda glad to see you, too."

I took a big whiff. My flak jacket reeked with the smell of death and destruction.

All of us hit the rec center. I battered the punching bag until my arms quivered. We drug ourselves back to the barracks.

Josh and I both had several letters from Jules waiting for us along with a box of her famous oatmeal cookies. No such luck as keeping these to ourselves. Suddenly I was starving. Josh and I grabbed a couple before passing them around.

Chapter 7

Schools Out

Fighting the heat, sometimes the bitter cold, and endless dust storms, only served to add an extra edge to the engagements with Taliban insurgents.

Every pile of garbage, stack of wares or anything lying around could be rigged with an explosive device. Often we would go out on patrols to uncover unexploded IED's (Improvised Explosive Devices). On my first discovery of an IED, I was so proud to have cleared the area, safely...only to find the next day a new IED found itself in nearly the same place. It became impossible to clear one site, secure it and move on.

Shortly before being redeployed, Martinez, one of the guys in our platoon, stepped on an IED. While the explosion didn't kill him, he went home without his left leg. Usually nothing happened, but those eventless occasions didn't lessen the danger or erase earned paranoia that kept us constantly vigilant.

Many times our patrols met with nothing but little children giving us hugs at the schools we helped reopen. Some weekends we picked up a game of soccer with the local boys. While other times the schools were dangerous places – especially the girl's facilities.

Santos and I approached one such girls' school in a small village nestled in a dusty community against the barren landscape. Cole and Hayworth came up behind us.

We were familiar with the school, as we had helped build it. We knew some of the teachers and remembered the cute little girls, heads covered in blue and white scarves, little angels marching in, some of them for their first day of school, ever.

Recently there had been several instances of school girls found tortured, families so warned not to send their girls to school. There had even been an incident in another village where nearly a hundred students plus several teachers had been poisoned. A few survivors were still in the hospital recovering.

The street seemed eerily quiet. There were only two heavily garbed women ambling along, glancing from side to side and over their shoulders. I signaled my team, quiet, and pointed. The team crouched behind a bombed out car, leaving the Afghan forces scattering between buildings.

Abreast, four Taliban surveyed the area, rifles rotating as they turned their attention to any noise or movement. They were headed directly for the school.

Without speaking, the men harassed the two women with their guns. The women huddled together in fear, gathered their long bhurkas as they shuffled off between the buildings.

Assessing the problem, I squinted in the bright sun watching the unsuspecting girls through an open window as they sat reading their books, silent soldiers fighting a literary battle for their education. I felt like a giant defending their right to be there. The Taliban men drew closer and closer.

When one man raised his AK47 aiming toward the open window, I squeezed off a volley of fire that riddled the gunman. Young screams pieced the air as he dropped forward suspended half way through the window. My team backed me up leaving the wall with another assassin heaped against it.

Return fire pitted the ground causing us to dive for cover. I felt one round whiz close to my head, when the air exploded in gunfire.

Suddenly dead silence sucked my breath away. Ahead lay a pile of the gunmen slumped against the wall and one sprawled on the ground.

I spotted Santos. A small girl clung to his leg. Hayworth, was across the street. Where was Cole?

I glanced over my shoulder. There he was, flat out in the middle of the street.

"Cole!" I put my hand on my heart, feeling it practically beating out of my chest.

I raced over and dropped to the ground beside him. I checked for a wound, a sign of blood. None. I touched the side of his neck. "Ok, Josh. You're alive." I leaned down. "Where are you hit, Buddy?"

Slowly his hand rose to his chest. He opened his eyes. He pulled the St. Christopher's medal out of his flak jacket and held it up. A gouge scarred the Saint Christopher's medal where the bullet ricocheted off it.

"Looks like...you didn't get rid of me yet," he sounded weak. "Feels like I got pummeled...with a baseball bat to the chest."

I helped him sit up. "Apparently between the vest and the medal you'll be back for another battle."

Staring upward, I said, "Thanks, God."

I was grateful He had been there watching over us all. No one was injured.

Chapter 8

Camp Alder Dunes

It wasn't long before we were on our way stateside. We returned to Camp Lejeune, North Carolina. Redeployment meant some education classes, thorough checkups and a re-evaluation. All of the guys in our squad had made it through in good health. While we had all experienced fear when awakened in the night with loud noises and some nightmares. Even so, none of our squad had succumbed to PTSD, where those sensations become reality. Deemed fit, we would train to get back in shape for another tour in Afghanistan.

Josh went home to Jules for a month's leave.

I home went too. I could hardly wait to see Beast. He met me in the hallway at my house, wagging his rear end so his tail banged against the walls. I couldn't help noticing that his gait had slowed. He made a half attempt to leap up before I dropped to the floor and jostled around with him. Beast and I spent my first week home sleeping until noon. It was so great to spread out on a king-sized bed, plenty of room even with Beast pressed against my back.

I spent some late nights out drinking with some high school buddies. They annoyed me - a little hard to listen to them complaining about how hot it got yesterday when the temp hit 82 degrees or how boring it is to live in Florence.

On Friday, Jules suggested all three of us go camping like we did when we kids. She decided on Alder Dune campground. Not only was it a place where Don had taken us all to fish when we were growing up, she emphasized there were some geocaching places she had never found before. She wanted to get us into her thing. "It's like hunting for treasure. Someone hides a little trinket in a secure package or box somewhere a little bit difficult to find. Then they input the GPS coordinates online, and we geocaching nuts go out searching for them." She had me talked into it.

Josh and Jules picked up the food. I packed my Jeep with all the supplies plus our gear. We took off the next morning at 7AM with Beast taking a big share of the back seat along side of Josh. Jules rode shotgun up front with me.

Traveling up the coast, a mere 5 or 6 miles, the fog broke into patches and the sun was burning a hole in the clouds allowing blue sky to dominate as we turned west into the campground.

Situated between Dune Lake and Alder Lake in the lush green Siuslaw National forest the campsites were all secluded by walls of native shrubs with thick Douglas fir. The green so contrasted with the scenery we had left in Afghanistan.

Jules and Josh set up their pop-up tent while I set up my one-man tent opposite theirs, overlooking Dune Lake. After that chore, we grabbed our fishing gear and hustled down to the lake, with Beast loping after us.

Jules had always tried to tag along when we were kids. Her first time accompanying us she got the royal initiation. After fishing for a while we returned to camp to clean the fish with Jules going, "Eeeeyou," scrunching up her face. Josh and I each scooped up a handful of fish guts then chased her around with the dripping entrails.

Now that we were grown, Jules could fish as well as one of the guys and had no trouble cleaning her own catch. Thus the art of fish-gut chasing had lost its allure.

That day Jules hooked the first fish. She had no sooner cast, than the fish bit, hauling her line out before she was ready. She scrambled around with her rod until she got it under control. She reeled him in like a pro. Beast sat up trying to help by snapping at the jiggling fish suspended above him.

"No, Beastie Boy. Down. This is my fish." She plopped the silvery trout into the bucket before hanging the bucket on a branch. "There, Beastie, no fish for you right now."

Next Josh got lucky. Grinning, he held his fish up as it dangled and twisted in the air.

"Mine makes yours look puny," Jules bragged. She reached for the bucket lifting her trout and holding it up for us to compare, then stretched up to hang the bucket over a branch. "Safe from you Beastie Boy."

"Yeah, well just wait," I said casting out into the still waters, sending circles of water waves around the line.

And wait we did because our laughter probably scared the fish away.

We ate the fried chicken and potato salad that Jules brought for lunch.

When we were just about to give up, I finally caught one. "Yeah, now we're talking fish!" I held up mine up, tail still flapping and spinning on the end of my line. "Loser cleans the fish," I said.

Back at camp, I brought the wood from my Jeep. While I built a fire, Josh cleaned the fish. However, this time, Jules scooped up the fish guts and chased me around the campsite. Josh caught her, knocked her off balance until she fell where Josh promptly started tickling her until she dropped the fish innards. Pay back was fair.

Recovered from her trouncing, Jules spread a cloth out on the picnic table, setting out plates and the last of the potato salad. She melted some butter in the pan, placed the fish side by side then sprinkled them with salt and pepper.

Sizzling in the pan, the scent filled the air, tantalizing our appetites.

"Throw me a beer," Josh said, sitting down next to Jules.

I tossed one over then popped one open for myself. "Beats those MREs," (Meals Ready to Eat.) I said, as I tasted the first bite of the lake trout. Beast waited for his tidbits.

We sat around the fire telling old stories, singing camp songs with beast howling along, roasting marshmallows and making Smores. It was like old times and I relished the lifelong friendship we forged stronger every time we spent time together.

The next day, we hiked. Jules brought her GPS and we hunted Geocaches, along the way. Searching for a "treasure" that someone hid, was more fun than I thought it would be though a whole lot less 'exciting' than locating IEDs. After a long search, I found a small metal box inside an old hollow log. I jumped up hollering, just like a kid who found a twenty-dollar bill. Jules signed the sheet and left her own little frog charm inside the container. I wondered how many of these caches were hiding, apparently all over the world.

They say you can't go back, but that camping trip was mighty close.

The next time all three of us were together would be totally, so totally different. And our lives would be forever changed.

Chapter 9

A Tragic Loss

It must seem strange to our friends back home, but being deployed again in Afghanistan was almost like going home, at least I returned to a familiarity, quite different than our arrival on the first tour. We got reacquainted with guys we hadn't seen for a while and checked out the new rec facilities.

When I saw Haseeb still there, we greeted each with a shoulder block, warm handshake and huge grins. It was good to see that our training of the Afghan Security forces was ongoing, leaving us with the perception that our withdrawal would not leave their country unguarded from the Taliban.

"How's it goin'?"

He caught me up on a lot of reconstruction and projects that took place in our absence. Sadly, two of the Afghan guys in the Security Guard had lost their lives.

We hadn't been back more that a month when we got some Intel that the Taliban held a family hostage. There had been sniper fire from the second story window for a couple hours. Our Marine team, Hayworth, Cole, Santos and I, joined with Afghan Security Forces to root them out.

As our Humvee approached the neighborhood of sandstone houses, lined up, blending into the surrounding desert, live ammo fire pinged off the hood. We pulled up behind a burned-out truck, checked our weapons. Silently we piled out under cover of the Afghan truck that had followed closely behind us.

Dashing to the side of the target area, a volley of fire sent patches of sand exploding around and between us. No one was hit as the swirl of dust blockage gave us temporary shield.

The Afghans provided cover fire as the four of us made our way toward the dusty two-story building. I approached the front, followed by several Afghans, while Cole took a position as a sniper in an adjacent building. I inched my way to the doorway ducking behind a shot-riddled car. Then I flattened my body and sidestepped against the wall. For a moment the silence was deafening. Hayworth sidled up behind me. We froze. Watching and listening for any movement, it came suddenly when burst of ammo flew through the air again.

Amid the volley of fire, I kicked open the door. I felt the bullet whiz by my ear. The Taliban next to me fell. The barrel of an AK-47 faced me. I ducked, grabbed the woman and child, dove over them, covering them on the ground with my body. The sound of gunfire was ear-splitting as bullets zipped overhead.

When the air cleared, I rose from the floor in the dimly lit room. Cole had his M 16 rifle hooked around and choking the neck of the last Taliban standing. The woman and her son crouched, quivering against the wall where two motionless bodies lay strewn across the floor.

A gurgling sound came from behind me as I turned. Hayworth buckled to the ground. "Hayworth!" I dropped down beside him. Blood spurted for the wound to his neck. I pressed in on the wound and momentarily stemmed the flow.

Josh scooped up a cloth from the table. He rushed over jamming it in the wound then tied the cloth around Hayworth's neck. We managed to carry him to the Humvee. "You're gonna be all right," I said as we loaded him in. "We'll get back soon. I'm right here."

"Step on it." We swerved causing a wake of sand spraying behind us as we rushed back toward base. I tried to hold Hayworth steady as we rumbled over the road. He kept trying to touch his breast pocket. A folded paper corner poked out of his flak jacket. I pulled it out just before his arm fell limply to his side. He was carrying a letter for his mom in his pocket.

"Hey, Santos, hang on to this." I handed him the letter.

The last thing Hayworth said was, "Mama." The kid was only 19. I cradled Hayworth in my arms.

This being the first time I had lost a friend, I wasn't prepared for the nausea that swept over me as I hung my head over the side spilling my guts into the sand.

It was weeks before I'd hit the rec center for anything other than vigorous exercise. I finally found solace by hitting golf balls off the roof of the supply building.

I never checked to see if the Taliban survivor ever made it into the truck or back to camp.

Chapter 10

We're Rescued

Returning to the barracks, facing the emptiness of our team without Hayworth, landed a devastating blow.

Jules second grade class had been writing to us. Opening the box sent the pack of Christmas crayon drawings scattering across the floor. They were hung up wherever we could find a space. For gifts, the children had sent us a bunch of batteries we could use in our electronic devices. But even their Christmas cheer couldn't evoke a smile when we stepped into barracks for the first time after Hayworth left us.

Even now I find it difficult to say dead or killed.

We spent a mighty somber night, much of it in silence. The next morning fared no better.

After I hit the head the next morning, I noticed a bucket next to the tent nearly eclipsed in the shade. It looked like a bucket of dirt. "What the..." I was drawn to the bucket when I saw a slight movement. I wasn't armed so I approached with caution. As I examined it, a puppy turned his humanoid blue eyes upward and captured mine. He lay coiled into a ball that just fit the circumference of the pail. Sometimes the enemy booby-trapped dogs, because the Americans acted so sappy over them. With many Afghans inside the compound, we were never sure if they were friendlies or ones who could be turned. Still I kept walking slowly toward the bucket.

He was so filthy.

What to do? If the dog were booby-trapped, I wouldn't be the only one blown to bits. I kept moving closer. I would have to do something; at least I needed to move the bucket away from the barracks.

Periodically a vector control squad came by to clear the area. If the kill patrol came along, the dog was a goner. Much as they tried to keep the wild packs of dogs out, dogs were still a danger. If this dog wasn't a member of their pack, the pack would kill it. A pack of wild dogs might even attack a person.

Dead dogs could be found everywhere, because the Afghans both hated and feared dogs. Children used them as target practice for their rock throws. I had seen men kick dogs mercilessly. I started to interfere once, but the dog tucked in his tail between his legs and slunk off to hide somewhere. There had been rumors that dogs were tortured, kicked, beaten, swung by their tails, even had their tails and ears chopped off.

Carefully, I picked up the bucket. Slowly I walked away from the encampment. I held my breath as I gently set the bucket in the sand. Then I knelt staring at frightened puppy. I couldn't see any device, but it could be planted underneath him. In slow motion, I lifted up the puppy. He kicked and yelped, begging me with his humanoid eyes.

Nothing! No hidden IEDs. We were safe, for the time being but not safe from the next predicament.

I stood for a moment weighing my options. A puppy didn't have much of a chance of survival without running with a pack of other dogs. If I decided to take him in, it could be a criminal offense since any pet could put soldiers in danger, not to mention the disease an animal might carry.

I'd have to conceal him somehow. You can see where my mind was headed.

I picked up the bucket and headed back. By the time I got near the barracks, I felt a creepy-crawly sensation. The fleas were having a circus on my arm plus I could see that fleas weren't the only varmints infesting the pup. There were also ticks.

"Hey you jarheads." When the guys saw what I had, they stared wide-eyed.

"Langston? What are you going to do with him?" Santos said.

"Deflea the bugger!" I said holding the bucket away from the entrance. "Cole. Get me some gasoline."

He took off heading for the motor pool.

"You can't. That'll kill him." Someone yelled.

"No it won't. My mom gave me a dose when we had a lice epidemic at school. Burned a little bit, but she shampooed me right away. I lived. The thing is, the lice didn't. I came back to school when everyone else stayed home a week waiting for the medicine the doc prescribed to work."

I turned to Santos. "Get some water and soap. Warm water!"

"Kinda bossy for someone who could get us in a lot of trouble." However, Santos came back faster than the fleas could multiply, with a bar of soap in one hand and the bucket slopping over with water, in his other.

You'd have thought the puppy would have loved his wash down in nice warm water, considering how cold December could be. Wrong. He kicked and yipped all the way through. I cuddled him in my arms while I dried him off. Though he couldn't have been used to human touch, he began to nose under my hand, begging for more strokes.

Clean, fluffy and nearly dry, I put him on the floor. I didn't think he was more than five or six weeks old. Now, instead of dingy brown, he glowed, a white and black fur ball, with big paws. A black spot circled the left side of his face. White fur streaked up his nose.. His black body wriggled while the white tip at the end of his tail wagged back and forth. His ears – now there was something. They poked almost straight up then suddenly they would flop down, sometimes one up while the other drooped down. They seemed to have their own personality.

After I set him down, the puppy quivered for a moment,

every eye trained on him. Then he shook himself off. For the first time in many hours, everyone in the tent laughed, and they continued grinning and laughing while the puppy sniffed his way around, his tail nearly wagging off his butt like a paintbrush spreading cheer. His white front paws poked at a sock lying on the floor.

Nose twitching, the puppy sniffed his way over to a chip bag he spied. He nosed his way into a half gone bag of potato chips. Instantly he munched the chips away, then he shook his head from side to side as he pawed at the crinkling bag trying to extricate his snout. He scampered around, nosing into flak jackets, helmets, checking everybody's rack. My hands hung down so he snuzzed in and curled up against them. As I watched the faces and listened to the sound of laughter, I knew that this dog was going to rescue us all.

"Hey Snuzz-bucket. I bet you're really hungry, huh? Want something to eat?" I scratched behind his ears. As if he understood, he cocked his head to the side, one ear up, the other down as if to say. "Well, where is it?"

Cole ran here and there gathering up MRE's. He opened one and set it before the pup. The dog sniffed it very briefly and then dug in.

Santos emptied a water bottle into a coffee mug. The puppy slurped up the water, like he'd had nothing to drink for a week. When he licked the last drop, he alternately snuzzed, kicked, pawed and chased the empty water bottle around the floor, keeping the smiles plastered on all our faces. Everyone was already calling him Snuzz.

Operation Snuzz-Bucket was afoot.

After we rounded up food and water bowls, we set up a box, lined with a blanket, in a corner where we hid it with Flak jackets piled on blankets. We organized ourselves into the Poop, Pea Exercise Patrol - PE patrol. This proved to be no easy chore considering it had to be done like a spy mission, one man watching and the other patrolling on "PE".

When they came to take away Hayworth's belongings, it was

a dark dismal day. Then the most remarkable thing happened. We were all sitting around or lying there in a funk when Snuzz sniffed around noticing the things missing. He came to each one of us, leapt up on our rack and sat with us for a long moment, snuzzing beneath a hand until he was acknowledged with a caress, and at the same time soothing an anguished soul.

I dropped to my knees and whispered, "Thank you, Lord."

Santos had been the closest one to Hayworth. He lay with head turned away from us, but his sorrow was apparent. He kept wiping his eyes, his shoulders heaving. He had kept himself cool and detached until now. He was completely overcome. When Snuzz came to Santos, he hopped up, lying next to him waiting until Santos composed himself. When Santos sat up, Snuzz climbed on his lap. He stared at the puppy then he finally he began stroking. Appearing weary, Santos rose to leave and the pup tagged right along behind him. When they came back, Santos entered, laughing and jostling Snuzz in the air like a baby.

The guys would actually talk about things to Snuzz they never would have shared with even their buddies.

Christmas was the next day. Other than the turkey dinner for chow, there hadn't been much to look forward to that is until Snuzz arrived.

On that Christmas Eve, we bungee-corded an armature, built with wire, around a M16. We poked the butt into the bucket filled with sand. Then we cut some paper decorations, made chains like in elementary school, stood back and admired our Afghani Christmas tree.

All the guys scoured the grounds for toys for Snuzz. He loved the paper we wrapped around the Ping-Pong balls, tennis balls, golf balls and socks, as much as he loved the toys. When he'd finished the snack gifts, he shook the papers, pounced on them, dragged, chewed, rolled in them and played tug-a-war with us, keeping us all in stitches.

It was a good Christmas after all.

Snuzz was a Godsend, finding the humanity in our inhumane existence.

The problem still existed. How would we, could we keep Snuzz a secret forever?

Chapter 11

Boot Camp For Snuzz

It would be virtually impossible to keep Snuzz under cover and to keep all of us safe, unless Snuzz could be perfectly trained.

"You're in boot camp as of right now, understood Private Snuzz?" Snuzz tilted his head and gazed at me. "Sit!" I commanded using a hand signal as well. I pushed his rear down. He sat. I scratched his ears. "Good Boy." At some point in time he would need to obey without a spoken word. "Sit!" I commanded with the hand signal using loving pats and praise as a reward. We wouldn't have treats for him out on patrol. Surprisingly it only took a couple of times until Snuzz obeyed with one or the other command. "You are one intelligent puppy."

At the PX, I bought a bunch of shoestrings. I tied six of them together around Cole's finger. He looked a bit silly while I braided Snuzz a collar plus a leash. Then I could really begin to train him. We all knew he wouldn't make it if he couldn't be trained so everyone participated.

Afghan dogs were very smart. I guess they had to be. They would starve or die in this rugged weather, hostile population, not to mention the other dog packs if they couldn't use their wits. Snuzz was no different. He picked things up in just a few tries. After he learned the basic commands of sit, stay, play dead, quiet and run, the guys were trying all sorts of tricks; dance, pray, shake, hop – Snuzz, our home entertainment center. "Run, quiet, play dead, attack," were commands that could save his life and ours. Each command had a hand signal. Snuzz would even do his business on command, an absolute necessity as he accompanied us on patrols.

I managed to commandeer the remnants of an IED after one of our patrols. It wasn't long before Snuzz could find it anywhere I hid it. I figured if I could turn him into a sniffer dog, if he were discovered, there would be a reason not to kill him. That sniffing skill made him very useful during missions and patrols. Now we considered him qualified as a regular WMD (working military dog).

We were afraid if other platoons knew we had Snuzz they would report us, so Snuzz was a well-kept secret.

One day we were out, dodging here and there, on PE when I saw the CO coming.

"Run." I said softly to Snuzz. He took off to where we had taught him to hide inside an oil drum. "Get out of here, Mutt!" I called after him.

I saluted.

"That wouldn't have been a dog I saw you with?" the CO said.

"Sir! That would have been against regulations."

"Then I won't see it again."

"I hope not, Sir."

"Carry on." He walked away.

"Whew," I wiped my brow.

I guess our letters home had either been short, dire or non-existent, until Snuzz came into our lives. Jules and I had been writing back and forth when this one came.

"Dear Zack,

I am so glad to see from your letters that your attitude is changing, both you and Josh sounded like you wouldn't make it for another year, but now I know you can. Snuzz sounds like just the ticket!

I have a friend, Shawna, new to our teaching staff this year. She said her 3rd grade class would also like to write.

Could you give her some names of some of your buddies that would like to have pen pals?

Her address is below.

Love, Jules

Our families definitely noticed the change in our communications before and after Snuzz. Our CO noticed a difference in our performance, too, but never asked more about why.

And I noticed a difference before and after Shawna's letters came.

Chapter 12

Nothing's Fair

Fortunately we had Snuzz pretty well under wraps and under control. Plus he was good about taking care of himself. We had found people who would feed and PE Patrol him when we were on longer missions. He had an uncanny ability to understand that Afghanis were not his friends. He slept every night in my rack, inching me further out with his growth spurts.

Snuzz never tired of his searches for IEDs or going out on patrols. On a number of incidents, our sniffer dog had proved to be not only an accurate IED locator but also our protector, not the other way around.

After I disbursed the first pack of letters from Shawna's 3rd graders to another platoon, she began writing to me. I knew I liked her a lot from her letters. We were able to discuss authors we liked and compared notes about her pet. Even though it was a cat, the behaviors reminded me of Beast back home. Then her picture arrived. Wow. I had a pin-up picture. She smiled back at me, creating deep dimples, her chestnut eyes flirting. I could imagine her riding in my Jeep, top down, with that long blonde hair blowing in the breeze. I had received the letter with her picture a day before our team's next patrol.

Just outside a small village, our Humvee pulled up behind an old beat up junker of a car. Suddenly it swerved across the road, blocking our passage. When the car door opened and a man barreled out of there running at high speed, I jammed our vehicle in reverse and stepped on it. At a distance of about 30 or 40 feet, the junker exploded sending our Humvee spinning in an out of control then sliding along on two wheels. The guys hurled themselves to the far side bringing the other two wheels back down on the road. Finally we skidded to a halt in a cloud of dust. I let out a huge gasp of air, looking around assessing our situation.

The junker-bomber was nowhere in sight, but there were bits and pieces of it everywhere.

"Our hero!" Josh yelled clapping me on the shoulder. "That was skillful driving, Andretti."

Sometimes you don't realize the small miracles in life. It was like Jesus was there in the Humvee with us.

When we took the Humvee to the motor pool for repairs, the bottom chassis was riddled with shrapnel that had miraculously avoided the gas tank or other essential mechanisms. Amazingly, had the Humvee not risen up on two wheels, undoubtedly more serious injuries than a few sore muscles.

Back at our hooch, Snuzz practically wagged his tail completely off before leaping in my arms. With his increasing size, he nearly toppled me over. It was as if he knew how close I came to not returning at all. We wrestled around a bit, lots of licking and tummy rubs.

Was I ever so glad that Snuzz was there, after I read the letter from my mother?

Chapter 13

He's Gone

I held the letter in front of me, reading it again through my blurry eyes as I sat on my rack.

Dear Zack,

I have prayed about this and received an answer. I found this picture of you with Beast under the couch while I was vacuuming. So I knew that I would have to let you know. It wouldn't wait until you returned.

There's no easy way to tell you.

Last week, Beast walked around gasping. He was having a hard time breathing. He wasn't eating very much. At the vet's, Dr. Boseman said his heart condition was much worse. Beast was having congestive heart failure. He said that nothing could be done for him. He told me that if Beast stopped eating, it would be because while he ate he couldn't breathe. Beast started walking around not wanting to lie down. It meant that he wasn't getting the air he needed and was probably in pain. He hadn't eaten anything all day. At that point, I would have to decide to let Beast wait in agony to die or that he could be put to rest and out of his misery.

I am so sorry, Zack. What a hard decision, one of the hardest I have ever made. But Beast was pacing and breathing so erratically. My heart ached for him. I took him in last night. Dr. Boseman treated him with such compassion. I got to stay with him and I held him close to me while the shot was administered. He closed his eyes in such a gentle sleep. I felt him finally relax his raspy breathing. He's at peace, Zack.

I love you,
Mom

My boyhood friend, who was always there for me, was gone. How could I ever go home without him there to greet me? I had pictured that tail wagging greeting for months. Lying back down, I rolled over. I couldn't hold back the tears. And there came Snuzz, finding his way into my arms.

That afternoon it happened, what I feared became a reality. The CO discovered Snuzz's water bowl.

"I thought we discussed this, Langston."

"Yes, Sir."

"You know what this means?"

"No, Sir."

That's when Snuzz came right up. He snuzzed against then licked his hand.

"Have you been keeping him in there with you?"

I kept my eyes zeroed in on his as though I could explain how much this dog meant to every man in our platoon with only a penetrating stare. "Yes, Sir."

"He can't stay."

"I know, Sir."

"Is that clear?" With a crooked smile he walked on.

"Yes, Sir." I let out a huge breath of air. It was perfectly clear. He was not going to follow through with reporting this to vector control. As soon as he turned the corner out of sight, I leaped up, hammering the air with my fist. "YES!"

From then on we allowed Snuzz a bit more freedom to come and go. He accompanied us on more of our patrols. While not allowed in any military vehicles, he was part of our no buddy left behind. If it was possible, Snuzz went along. No one reported us.

Snuzz took to sleeping in the day when he didn't go out on patrol. At night he'd keep watch. After coming out, one night to hit the head, a pack of dogs had killed something. I seemed to be in their way, a threat to the finishing of their meal. Baring their teeth and growling, I faced about six feral dogs seemingly bent on taking me out of their way. That's when Snuzz stepped in front of me matching them growl for growl. The dogs backed off so Snuzz let me start walking backward while he continued to stare down the pack. He turned to walk back, stopping, bracing, growling with a deadly snarl.

What we hoped was our last problematic patrol before going home from our tour, occurred as we were responding to a truck explosion on the road to Kandahar.

A roadside bomb had discharged. While the explosive device had missed its mark causing little damage and minor injuries, they needed forces to protect the supply convoy while the wreckage was cleared.

As we arrived, we set up a perimeter watch. We surveyed the area with binoculars. The only lump of foliage dotting the sandy horizon loomed off about 100 feet away. I thought I saw some movement. Then, in my peripheral vision, I spotted a man approaching Cole where he stood in conversation with an Afghan security guard. I turned. The turbaned man walked slowly toward them with his arms our stretched. The dusty wind whipped his baggy clothing. I thought I detected some sort of IED strapped beneath his waistcoat.

"Halt," I yelled with my rifle leveled at his head. "Stop or I'll shoot."

He continued walking toward us. I ground the dust between my teeth. "Halt!" When he reached toward his IED, tottered ahead and shouted, "Allah..." my bullets weren't the only ones riddling the terrorist's body, contorted and snapping as the volley of fire penetrated. In the same instant he exploded, I dove for Josh knocking him to the ground. The boom was thunderous. We sat up dazed, engulfed in the foul smelling smoke.

My ears rang. In my blurred vision I could make out josh mouthing, " Zack! Are you all right?" Josh shook me.

"Yeah, Yeah," I responded as some of the ringing subsided and I could see more clearly.

"Your foot is bleeding." I pointed.

He glanced down as though he didn't even notice. We helped each other up as we took stock of the damage. Fortunately the IED had exploded far enough away to do little damage accept for the shrapnel. Head high, right about where Josh had stood, a large piece of shrapnel had ripped into the truck. I helped Josh into one of the trucks where they were loading the injured. Josh wasn't the only one hit, but he and the three others had relatively minor wounds.

No fatalities with two bombs exploding.

As I leaned into the truck, the smell of the oiled canvas stretched over the top of the truck bed blended with the smell of disinfectants applied to the wounded.

Josh took out his St. Christopher's medal and kissed it. "My ticket outta here!"

The injury proved lucky for Josh, not only because the shrapnel didn't take him out, but he went home on leave to recoup before returning to finish the last three months of his tour of duty.

After a few of these missions, it didn't take much to realize; we were there fighting for our country, though more importantly, we were all there for each other.

When I got back to the base, I had a package waiting for me from Mom – a large jar of peanut butter. Wow! My popularity with Snuzz soared. After the rest of us finished most of it off, Snuzz adopted the nearly empty jar. It kept him busy for at least an hour while he pushed it around the floor, held it in his paws and licked the heck out of it.

Snuzz followed me everywhere especially on missions where

we needed his expertise at sniffing out IED's. One day I was truly lucky I took him along. We were patrolling a blind alley where a Taliban trained his weapon on me from a recessed doorway. Snuzz tore down close to the wall and was on him like flies on crapola. He leaped up literally chomping on the man's rifle, tore it out of his hands then pounced him to the ground with his teeth pressed around his victim's throat. You should have seen the man plead when Snuzz was more than snuzzing his jugular and snarling an ominous guttural snarl. We kept him very busy.

Snuzz became so much a part of our daily lives. He was a member of our platoon, one of us. He saved our lives not only with his bravery, but also by being there when we needed a silent friend to listen to us. I wasn't the only one who took him on long walks while we spilled our guts out to him. He was a silent friend who brought sanity to a barren desolate place, laughter with his antics and howling when we let off steam.

One day I realized that we had only a few months before we went home. Redeployment, we all talked about it waiting in great anticipation. What we hadn't thought about was Snuzz. It wasn't an option to leave a Marine behind.

When the CO turned down our request to take him home with us, doom descended on everyone's shoulders.

Chapter 14

Now What To Do?

I had to do something. There were stories about a few pets that had made it stateside from Iraq with some from Afghanistan, too. I was going to make that rumor come true.

On top of that, there were rumors that research was complete insuring that the production of a technical device that could detect IEDs would be stepped up. Though some dogs might be retained for sniffing HMEs, homemade bombs made from fertilizers, sniffer dogs would soon be replaced by the electronic sensor, purported to be more effective than dogs.

Snuzz would have little practical use if we left him behind.

My first reaches were to Shawna, Jules and Mom during our Skype phone calls.

When Josh returned from leave, I began to feel hope. Shawna called. She saw a program on FOX TV about pets being rescued out of Iraq through the SPCAI, the Society for the Prevention of Cruelty to Animals International, and their Operation Bagdad. I had the concrete evidence that Snuzz had a chance.

I immediately went on line. In fact, while more pets had been rescued through the SPCAI from Iraq, that some indeed, had come home from Afghanistan. On further investigation I found contact addresses with phone numbers. The guys standing around me let out yelps and cheers like we won the BCS National Championship.

It was a bit premature for cheering. I talked to a man in Washington DC from the SPCAI, international SPCA, who assured me they would go to great lengths to help me bring Snuzz home.

After I contacted the SPCAI, I learned there were obstacles, huge obstacles, to overcome. First Snuzz would have to be screened, vaccinated, and carry health certificates issued by veterinarians along the way through each country of departure. Before he even left this sand pit, the minister of Agriculture might have to issue travel papers.

The dog would need to be transported to Islamabad, Pakistan, approved, certified, after which he'd be transferred to an aircraft to proceed to England. From there, Snuzz would board a plane for home.

How would we get the dog to Islamabad?

While it wasn't hundreds of miles, we could not use military vehicles for anything other than routine patrols or when we were assigned to special missions.

Slump shouldered I digested those bits of news before chewing on the issue of money. It could cost thousands of dollars.

That afternoon, the guys sat around brainstorming. Snuzz sat perfectly still while Santos' pencil scratched across a piece of paper resulting in a sketch that bore a pretty good resemblance to him.

Meanwhile, several solutions for our predicament

materialized.

Money? The SPCAI offered to help set up a bank account where donations could be made.

Operation Bring Snuzz Home had begun.

First we organized a group of us to be filmed for our debut into the world of YouTube. Our artistic endeavor included a repertoire of Snuzz tricks. He rolled over. He rose up on his back legs hopped over to me and then danced to iPhone music. We sang while he yowled and yipped along with the song. He shook hands with us and licked our faces. For his finale, he leaned against my rack, his paws pressed together, praying, "Please Lord, make it possible for me to come home," which I intoned in my finest raspy dog voice. The guys held up a sign indicating where the donation checks could be sent.

We emailed and Face-booked everyone we knew.

The hits came in immediately, but would the checks?

There was a vet attending the official sniffer dogs. Could he be persuaded to vaccinate Snuzz?

The next morning I went to his office.

"I'm sorry but regulations prohibit me from treating your dog. You know that."

"But, Sir." No amount of explaining could change his mind.

He shook his head. "I'm sorry. I can't help you."

After hitting the rec hall and beating a punching bag for an hour, I went back to my laptop. It was late in the US so I emailed my DC contact at the SCPAI. How long would it be before he told me we'd just have to forget it? I couldn't tell the guys. I slept a fitful, toss and turn night.

Time ticked away. There was only a small window of time when weather permitted the transport of animals in aircraft that didn't have a temperature controlled hold. They extended the deadline due to an unusually warm fall. If we couldn't arrange it prior to the dead line date, we'd have to wait. If we waited, we would be redeployed. There was no guarantee that Snuzz would be a priority to anyone other than our platoon when we were stateside.

Very early the next morning, the CO woke me before dawn. "Get up and get that dog to the vet! Now!"

"Sir?"

"The SPCA International contacted me last night. I was very persuasive with the Doc. He said if you were over there in 20 minutes, he'd vaccinate the dog."

"B...But how..."

"Let's just say I've known him for a long time." He raised an eyebrow. "I know some things he'd rather I forgot."

"I...I don't know how to thank you, Sir."

"Just get the damned dog over there!"

"Yes, Sir!" I said pulling up my pants and tripping over to my boots.

"He's also getting travel papers from the Minister of Agriculture."

My heart was pounding in my chest even before I started running. In minutes I took off, Snuzz racing behind me. We had a very important appointment.

The vet finished up an examination.

"Dog looks pretty healthy." He prodded a little more and examined Snuzz's ears. The Doc gave him the shots while I held him. "I understand you did pretty well funding this little covert operation."

"Sir?"

"Ask your CO."

Apparently YouTube was the miracle we needed. The plane trip to the US was nearly paid for.

I kind of wondered who they'd have to pay off to swing all this.

Next we needed to arrange the transportation to the airport. After trying every angle I could without letting the wrong people know what I was up to, no one would give us orders to take any vehicle of any kind to Islamabad. The alternative was to go to Kabul, only about 30-mile trip, and arrange a flight to Islamabad.

Even my CO couldn't help me.

The weather was holding but how long did we have until the airlines refused to take any more animals.

One afternoon while in my deepest funk, The SPCAI contacted me about an Afghani who offered to pick up Snuzz. He'd take him to Kabul where the SPCAI had arranged flight to Islamabad.

"I just want to let you know this is not a sure thing."

"What do you mean?" I sank back on my chair.

"I am going to give you the man's name and contact information. You must not mention this or his name to anyone. He is putting his life in danger."

"Why would he do this?"

"Why does anyone do something like this?"

"I know why you're doing this, Sir, but an Afghani?"

"The money's only worth it if your dog isn't discovered. You understand. The man will dump him, if there's any suspicion of danger."

My throat closed and my chest tightened.

"You need to build him a regulation dog kennel. Check on the Internet. In England we'll switch him into a ready-made."

"Okay."

"It needs to be done in the next day or two. Contact our man. He knows when he has to get the dog to the airport. Oh, and make sure the dog has all the travel papers."

I gulped. I still didn't have everything from the vet.

"Can you do it?"

"I'll have to. Thank you so much."

From the beginning people told me that there were plenty of successful missions in rescuing dogs from Iraq. However there were only a few dogs and one cat that had made it home from Afghanistan. Animals could be lost along their way.

I let the guys know what was happening after I contacted the

Afghani.

Josh scratched Snuzz behind the ears then hooked his arm around my neck. "Don't worry guys. The SPCAI knows what their doing."

A wave of perspiration broke over my forehead. Snuzz would be gone in two days. Could I actually trust a person known to come from a culture that holds dogs in such disdain?

Would I ever see Snuzz again?

Chapter 15

A Road Less Traveled

The CO must've been on the Doc's case because the travel documents came though the next day while we were constructing Snuzz's travel kennel. We rigged up a plastic water bottle with plastic tubing that wouldn't spill, was easy to refill and that Snuzz could lick at will. We assembled food to be stored in the labeled compartments we built.

I had to trust that security details in the various airports would take Snuzz out for PE, make sure he had food and water. It would be a rough week until we learned that all had proceeded according to plan.

We practiced getting Snuzz in and out of the crate. That was no easy chore at first. There was a whole lot of power in those legs when he braced his paws against the frame refusing to go in. Food proved to be the ultimate persuader. Soon he stepped in with only a backwards glance asking, "Are you sure?" The final loading in would be the hardest, at least for all the guys.

The following morning at 0500 Snuzz said his last goodbyes. As though he sensed the finality of this, he visited each man, got his hug and snuzz. Most of the guys were wiping their eyes or turning away while it was my turn. Snuzz lay down looking up at me. "Tummy rub, you big old boy. I'm gonna miss you." I massaged him all over. "So, so much."

I led him over to the cage, he rolled his sad blue eyes in my direction as if he said, "Do I have to?"

"Yes, Buddy, you have to." I thought my heart would beat

out of my chest. What was that running down my cheek? I reached up and wiped my face.

After I snapped the door shut and locked it, Snuzz whined, and gave a pitiful anguished, "ar" that held for the longest minute. Then he laid down, head on his paws, eyeing me.

How could just saying goodbye to a dog be this painful?

The Afghan stood by his rickety truck, while we loaded the crate into the back. I showed him the hand signals he'd need, "quiet" or "run" being the most important. For a visual, I had drawn pictures of the commands for people who might encounter Snuzz along the way. The Afghani looked me in the eye, stuck out his hand for a shake. I grasp it and shook, hoping that the plaintive expression in my eyes would tell him how important his mission was. He smiled a crooked grin exposing two gaping holes where teeth had once resided - a sneer or a smile?

The man threw a ragged blanket over the kennel, climbed in the cab, and rumbled off toward the gate.

Santos filmed this with his phone. YouTube fans needed to know what they accomplished.

Operation Bring Snuzz Home wouldn't be over until he set his paws in my house back in Florence, Oregon.

Empty. Empty hearts. Empty barracks.

Chapter 16

Home is Where the Heart Is

I had no idea how much my CO had to do with Snuzz getting to the airport in Kabul, seeing to his PE and getting him stowed on board. A simple, "thanks," is all he could receive since the whole operation violated regulations. So we knew almost immediately when Snuzz landed in Islamabad by the next day.

What we wouldn't know for two very long days is what had happened in Islamabad.

I got a call from SPCAI. "We had a problem."

"Snuzz. Is he okay?"

"Well, finally. They left him in the hangar over night before anyone came to check on him. He was pretty dehydrated. Fortunately we had a contact who followed through, cleaned up everything plus made sure he had food and water."

"Good." I said through clenched teeth.

"We had another problem…"

"What now?"

"The contact scrambled around trying to find a vet who would stamp the dog's travel papers."

"Tell me he's not stuck in Islamabad."

"Not any more."

"So now what?" My hands were shaking.

"He's on his way to London. He arrived a day late, but we were able to reschedule a flight to New York."

"But … But my mother is going to be waiting in Washington DC," my voice rose in pitch.

"She's been in contact with us. She's driving to New York and will pick your dog up at JFK."

"There will be a little tie up when he arrives in New York. He has to be screened as well as be approved for entrance into the US by the CDC.

"What's that?"

"The Federal Center for Disease Control."

"Sounds like another big hurdle."

"It was, the first few times we carried out a mission like this, but now it has almost become routine."

"I can't believe this is really happening."

"It is young man. It's been my pleasure to do this. We feel strong in our support of the troops and their sacrifice for our country. It's our way of thanking you. It's the least we can do."

Celebration time at chow that evening! We knew the journey wasn't over, but chances of things getting hung up now seemed less than the first leg of this operation.

It had been decided that it might be a fun trip for Mom to drive cross- country to pick up Snuzz. Since Jules and Shawna were on Thanksgiving break from teaching, they offered to accompany her. Their trip would make it easier rather than routing Snuzz through O'Hare with another plane transfer and a third airport in Portland.

From the parking lot of JFK, Mom's call reached me so we conversed on our iPhones. Modern technology was never more appreciated than when I saw Snuzz with all of my favorite women, together having such a good time.

The guys gathered around trying to peek over my shoulder.

"I think he loves all you girls," I grinned.

"How can you tell?" Jules knelt down with her arm around Snuzz. He was doing a great job of washing the makeup off her scrunched up face.

"That's my wife!" Josh yelled as he jabbed the air pointing.

"I worried how Snuzz'd react after being with nothing but guys. So in case he gets too rambunctious, let me show you a few of his commands."

The girls were smart. They brought a bunch of dog treats. He'd never had any treats like that before. It didn't take much to see they were becoming near and dear to Snuzz's taste buds. All I had to worry about Snuzz right now was about how fat he'd be by the time I got home.

After they practiced a few hand and voice commands, I knew Snuzz wouldn't give them his ration of...sh...misbehavior. I handed the phone to Josh who had a few mushy things to say while we all stood back.

They say, "Home is where the heart is." I knew exactly were my heart was.

Making it safely through a month and a half until we'd be redeployed became the next concern on our minds.

With only a little over a week left, our squad was ordered on a mission to take out a compound of IED producers. Nerves were on edge, since we were such short timers. We had heard rumors that two years before we arrived, the majority of a platoon had been wiped out just days before they were redeployed.

Chapter 17

Last Hurrah

An intercepted message indicated that the Taliban had taken over an abandoned building where they were manufacturing IED's. That meant we'd find plenty of firepower and this could be a very dangerous mission. We were being assigned to take out the site, though we had no intel on how many Taliban might be involved or how extensive the operation was.

It could also be a trap or erroneous info.

I promised God I would forever be in His service, if He would just bring us all back from this mission safely.

In full MCU (Marine Combat uniform), the squad moved out at 1400 along with Afghan Security Forces. We were on site about an hour later.

We came to a rise overlooking the "bomb plant". That rise provided us some cover to set up the operation. Located within the required 250-meter range, Cole set up the SMAW (Shoulder-Launched Multipurpose Assault Weapon). He attached the spotting rifle which, when fired with the rocket launcher, insured deadly accuracy. Cole lined up the target. Hand held high, he gave us the thumbs up.

While the building wasn't entirely isolated, the two-story structure faded into the drab landscape situated about 100 yards from any other structures.

We set up the perimeter.

Prayers blaring from outside speakers called the Muslims to prayer. We had to wait until the four bomb builders marched out, spread their rugs, and dropped to the ground facing Mecca. At least the ritual prayer furnished us information of how many Taliban were in the building. The drone of the prayers continued, while we waited, hunkering behind our bunker waiting for the minutes to drag by. After we returned home, I hoped it would be a very long time before I heard this prayer call again.

Darkness began to overtake the clear deep blue sky. It wasn't a full moon but enough light glowed down to increase the danger.

This could be an easy mission, if our team wasn't detected on recon verifying the location, its occupants, and the suspected use of the building. A mistake in target could cause giant repercussions in American-Afghan relations not to mention the consequences for those deemed responsible for an error.

Small dry bushes dotted the sandy terrain and created movement in the brisk wind. The landscape plus the small rises and drops in the sandy surface provided some cover for our descent. We attached brush to our helmets. My heart raced. I prayed our camouflage efforts would be effective. Our night goggles afforded us an advantage over the Taliban; so we might not need to get extremely close to verify our suspicions. I clicked mine in place and signaled my team.

Santos and Haseeb circled east while I slid down the sandy embankment to the west.

On our bellies, we elbowed our way along holding the M16s out-stretched out in front of us. How often had we found this undesirable part of our basic training an essential maneuver in accomplishing an objective?

We were able to rise up and crab-walk a small distance to the next rise, before we hit the sand again. I brushed the dust out of my nose and mouth. I elbowed ahead.

I froze.

An Afghan slid open the wide entrance door to the building allowing a triangle of light to illuminate the flat expanse of ground that stretched in front of me. He raised a pair of binoculars to his eyes and surveyed the horizon from side to side.

Inching out of the light into the shadow of night, I checked the man's line of vision. I could not see the rest of the squad as they spread out over the rise, though I knew their weapons were at the ready, waiting for my signal.

I scanned the hill. I could see Santos though not Haseeb. Had they been they detected by the enemy?

The man ducked inside without sliding the door closed.

I crawled down close enough to see inside. There were three other men assembling materials that were obviously IED's.

That's when the man stepped back through the doorway. He leveled his machine gun at Santos and Haseeb, let loose, strafing the area in front of my buddies. As the sand blasted in the air, they took off running up and dove over the rise.

After I took out the shooter with a couple of rounds, I jammed it in high gear over the edge, continuing up toward the squad.

I gave Cole the signal.

Knowing I had a few seconds to clear some more ground before I turned back to watch the fireworks, I scrambled up the sandy rise.

They never saw it coming. Cole launched the rocket that blasted into the building with his usual accuracy. The initial firestorm escalated as it plowed into the explosives stacked inside. A huge orange mushroom blossomed, lighting the sky as the lit shrapnel flew in all directions, exploding like the finale-sized fire works at a Fourth of July celebration.

A giant cheer rose from the men on the ridge as the remnants of brilliance showered down from the sky.

Finally I could see Santos and Haseeb joining the guys cheering, dancing around and slapping palms.

I hadn't realized I was holding my breath. When the air came streaming out, I felt like I would pass out, but I managed to make it back, light-headed, ears ringing, while engulfed in the foul-smelling cloud of smoke, but still there. "Thank you, Lord," I said as I gazed skyward.

Santos' cheek bled, grazed, though barely grazed, by the Taliban fire. All the guys teased him about the how the chicks would swoon when he pointed to his scar told them stories of his heroism.

This operation could have saved hundreds from the individual IEDs and HMEs that would never be detonated.

That night I experienced the nightmare. I relived the shooting of that man in slow motion, the angle of his face contorted in the realization of his plight, the agonized scream as my bullets exploded in his chest.

Sitting up, I broke into a sweat that left my body soaked. Grabbing my helmet, I threw up. I couldn't close my eyes so I lay there until dawn stretching my mind away from the thoughts of war.

Fortunately, the next days were filled with redeployment issues, packing up and bidding farewell to those who would be left behind. I concentrated on so many things to look forward to.

Finally we were on our way home, home in plenty of time for Christmas. My mind filled with the people I would see, reuniting with Snuzz, maybe even a prayer for little rain, as though rain could wash away the past months of combat.

Christmas came though this was definitely not the kind of Christmas I had played out in my mind.

Chapter 18
The Good Ol' USA

You have to miss something before you appreciate it. When the plane's wheels touched down at Raleigh Durham Airport, I was overwhelmed with appreciation for American soil and all that it meant.

Strangely the first thing I noticed while deplaning was a girl, though I wasn't checking out her obvious sensual body parts. It was winter. Even so, she wore these pink flip-flops. It had been a very long time since I seen a woman's naked feet. Her toes wiggled, drawing my attention to her toe rings and the bright red polish. I hadn't ever been into foot fetish before, but wow, what a turn on!

After settling in at the Camp Lejeune for final debriefing, thorough check ups and a re-evaluation, we prepared to go home on leave. We had one night in Jacksonville before our flight to Eugene, Oregon.

Josh called Jules. Our three-way conversation carried on for a few minutes. Then Josh took over with all that mushy stuff.

Every time we talked, I had a sudden rush of nostalgia for the way it used to be. Would it, could it ever be the same? I know I felt changed, like I was 35 instead of 25. In the back of my thoughts, I sure hoped Snuzz would remember me when I got home.

"What'll we do on our last night?" I asked Josh as he came away from his call.

"The bar at the Chili's has entertainment tonight," Gonzales, one of the local guys piped in. You want a ride? Me and Wells are going into town in a few minutes."

So we piled into the back seat of his Camaro.

"There'll be a game on the tube 'til the band starts," I said.

"Cheap Beer on tap, sexy waitresses." Gonzales cupped his hands out front of his chest. "Maybe I should come with you instead of seeing my Rosalie. On better thought - not."

When we got to Jacksonville, Gonzales pulled over to the curb to let us off on Market Street, across the street from the Chili's.

"We'll catch the bus back. See ya." Josh slammed the car door.

Across the street from us, the huge Chili's neon sign filled the sky with red and green neon light. We laughed while giving each other shoulder blocks as we ambled toward the bar.

Inside the cafe we made our way to the bar where some jarheads and locals stood around tossing 'em down.

"A great supply of women." I noted as we squeezed in close to the bar.

"Two drafts." Josh yelled.

"Three," I added when the big busted blonde stared up at me with her lash laden blue eyes.

"Hi, Soldier."

I ran my hand across my nearly bald regulation hair cut. It was almost impossible to blend into a crowd of locals even in our civvies.

She flipped a wave of corn-silk hair over her shoulder.

I put my arm around her waist. "So how come someone as gorgeous as you are is here by herself?"

"I dunno."

The beers came. Josh grabbed his and gave me a salute as he headed across the room for the pool tables.

"I'm Zack and you are…?" I handed her a beer.

"Renee." She dipped her index finger in the beer head, lifted it to her shiny lips, looked square into my eyes and licked away the froth in slow motion.

As the band started to play, she tapped her red fingernails on the bar while her hips rocked to the rhythm.

"Wanna dance?" I asked, though having other thoughts on my mind.

As she took my hand and led me out to the floor, I admired how her hips moved in the skin-tight jeans. The space between her jersey and the jeans revealed a peak of a long triangular tattoo spread on her backside, a landing strip, as the guys referred to those tattoos. I imagined her wearing only that tattoo.

On the crowded dance floor, with all the people jumping around, I was inhibited from showing off my svelte moves. Besides I was much to busy watching her undulating to the music while my mind worked overtime on how this evening could end. Maybe she had a car and maybe her apartment was close. Then there was Josh.

It turned out that she actually had driven with another girl who was the driver. I guess the night wasn't going to end in a finale like I imagined. Maybe I'd have figured out how it could meet my expectations if we weren't leaving the next day.

We danced a few more, but obviously, "I dunno", made up a big part of Renee's vocabulary.

So I ordered another beer and I left her for a hot game of pool.

Josh was in the midst of a game so I put my money up on the corner of the table. We had a lot of practice in Afghanistan at the rec center, but Josh, the sharpshooter proved he was just as good with a cue as he was with a weapon.

Josh ran the last few stripes and picked up his winnings. I selected my cue and racked 'em up.

"A little side bet?" He put up a five.

Sometimes he liked to hustle so I wondered if he planned on doing just that when I managed to bank the eight ball in before he could. I picked up the five.

That meant I had to play this dude who sidled up to the table, scratched his scrawny goatee, tipped his Panther's baseball cap back, sneered, and racked 'em. He broke and began running the table. I got two shots in before he finished me off.

When Josh stepped back and laid his twenty down, the big guy said, "You're on." He never saw it coming.

When his turn came, Josh ran the table and picked up his twenty together with his winnings.

"C'mon, Zack. This drink's on me."

We had a couple more beers before we decided to catch the last bus back to the base.

The mist began to fall. The bright lights from Chili's big green and red sign along with the other lights laid a shiny rainbow of streaks across the wet pavement. Triangles of light poured down from the overhead streetlights, shining the sidewalk.

The bus station was located a few blocks down so we rolled up our coat collars and started walking.

I saw a soda can lying there on the sidewalk next to the wall. So good to be home, in Afghanistan, a can could be the housing for an IED. It took a while to leave those fears behind. It was still the first thought in my mind as he reached for the can.

Josh swooped up the soda can. "Hey, go out for one."

I started running back as Josh blasted it as hard as he could. I went out for a short toss as the hollow can wasn't in the mood to sail very far. Josh ran after me trading a few shoulder blocks when we came to the cross walk.

Laughing and reminiscing about one of our last games with the Ducks, we weren't paying much attention to traffic as the streets were nearly empty that late.

As we stepped into the cross walk, out of nowhere came two headlights barreling toward us. I stood frozen like a deer caught highlighted in the middle of one of those Oregon back roads. The next thing I knew, I flew backward onto the sidewalk where Josh had shoved me.

"What the…" I stared up from my prone position.

The oncoming car barely braked skidding across the slick highway. It took a moment for me to understand what I was seeing –

what I was hearing. Like a slow motion movie sequence, the car rolled over Josh. I heard the double thud as first the front wheels rolled over him then the car's back tires pummeled him again.

I leaped up sprinting toward the lump on the ground. "Call 911!" I yelled at several people that had swerved over. People jumped out of their cars and rushed toward us.

Josh was covered in blood. His chest was crushed with legs splayed out at odd angles. I dropped next to him.

"Don't you dare bail on me now!"

"Hey…we're even…now," Josh gasped with a trickle of blood rimming his lips.

I stripped off my jacket, put it under his head then tried to assess his injuries.

"You're gonna be all right. An ambulance is on its way."

A woman came up and laid her coat over him.

"Tell Jules… Tell her… I love her," he whispered, choking it out. .

"You tell her…Damn it!"

Were his lungs filling with blood? CPR didn't seem like an option considering all the apparent injuries as well as those I feared.

I leaned close to his face. "Stay with me, Buddy."

"Give her…my medal."

I knew instantly he meant the St. Christopher's medal Juliana had given him before we went to basic training. He wore it constantly baring the ping mark marring its surface where the bullet glanced off it.

"Take care… of… her, Za..."

"Always."

His eyes rolled back into his head. His labored breathing ceased. "Come on Breathe!" My heart pounded. "Please God," I begged.

I held him in my arms and breathed into his mouth until the ambulance arrived then the EMTs took over.

That's when I noticed his St. Christopher's medal was on the ground. I scooped it up in my hand.

He was breathing again when they loaded him on the gurney. They cut away some of his clothing, passed me his dog tags before they attached the monitors.

"Everything's gonna be okay, Buddy." I wiped my eyes. "Gonna be okay."

I held his hand all the way to the emergency room, wearing mumbled prayers on my lips, with the St. Christopher's medal clenched between our palms.

Chapter 19

Going Home

The hospital smell hit me as soon as I walked through the double doors. I watched them transfer Josh to the gurney then roll him down the pristine sleek gray hallway toward surgery.

Alone in the corridor, I managed to pull my cell out to give Jules a call. I held the phone and stared as it lay in my bloodstained hands. I pressed in the number. This was my fault. Josh saved my life. Now he's…

"It's serious, Jules…" I explained. "…But he's going to be all right. He just has to be. I'll call you as soon as he's out of surgery."

I am not sure why, but the phone call to Josh's parents was even harder.

How long had I stood there, before sinking to the floor staring straight ahead? I rolled the St. Christopher's medal under my thumb. All the dangers we braved during our tour did nothing to prepare me for the utter desperation I felt. Not having Josh in my life was not an option. Knowing the extensive injuries the medics were able to patch up in Afghanistan, gave me hope. We were in the best conditions, with the best doctors, in the best hospital to save this very fit Marine.

An older man walked past. He must have noticed me slumped against the wall with the medal in my hands because he turned and came back. He bent over me. "Look. Why don't you get up from there? I'm on my way to the chapel. It would do you good to come with me."

I stared up blankly.

He reached his hand out. "Come on now."

I accepted his help up. Together we walked down the hallway.

"Who are you waiting for, Son?"

"My buddy. Car accident." I couldn't elaborate.

"My wife, she broke her hip. She's having emergency surgery. I'll pray for them both."

The small chapel immediately felt serene and comforting with its soft lighting and warm wooden pews. I slid in after the man.

Sitting there, for a long while, I felt ashamed that I only seemed to pray when I needed something. Still, I bent my head in prayer. "Please God, just this one more favor..." We sat in silence while the serenity calmed my nerves.

"Thank you," I said to man as I left. I wanted to make sure I was back when the surgery was over. The long hallway stretched ahead of me as I dragged myself back to wait. I sank into one of the institutional gray chairs in the waiting room, staring, letting the gray tweed carpet blur my thoughts, unaware of anyone else in the room.

Hours later, I heard footsteps from the hallway and stared at the blue booty shoe covers as the doctor softly entered the waiting room. When I looked up, Dr. Easton pulled the mask from his face. He ran his hand through a sweaty tangle of bushy steel hair. I stood and faced him. He didn't speak for a moment, but his eyes did.

It wasn't good.

"How bad is it? When can I see him?"

The doctor reached out and touched my shoulder. "He's gone, son. He didn't have a chance. We did all we could..." he glanced away then back at me. "...The injuries were too extensive." He held me at arms length while he stared into my eyes. "Are you going to be okay?"

I nodded.

"Shall I send for someone?"

"No." I swallowed. "I'll be all right."

He turned and walked away down the hall, slump shouldered. It wasn't until later when I realized that doctors must suffer greatly when they lose a patient. The doctor's eyes were brimming when he gave me the somber news. As I watched him disappear around the corner, I became cold all over. I couldn't breathe.

"No!" I screamed as I dropped to my knees holding my head in my hands. The memory of the bloody street flashed into my brain like a horror movie. For the first time, I saw the driver. It was a young woman who staggered over yelling and slurring, "I didn't see… him. I didn't mean it!" I had blocked her out because of my intimate moments with Josh. But it all came rushing at me like the glaring headlights.

I will always remember the smells of that night. The wet cement, the screeching burned rubber, the smell of Josh's aftershave mingled with sweat combined with the reeking alcohol from the woman who killed my best friend, my brother.

If we hadn't been drinking, if we hadn't been messing around, if only we came to that corner a minute earlier or a minute later. If only…

The phone lay next to me where it had dropped out of my pocket. Jules. She didn't know yet. I remember dialing, but I can't recall what I said to her. I do remember telling her I would call Don and Kelly. Josh's parents needed to hear it from me. Without a doubt, those were the two hardest calls I made in my life.

I felt light-headed as I approached the nurses' station. Grabbing for the counter I steadied myself. "Excuse me." A blonde curly haired woman turned and faced me, dropping her half-moon glasses, caught by the chain around her neck.

"Can I help you?" She shuffled closer smoothing down her blue smock.

"Uh. Is there…uh, my friend…d…didn't make it." Somehow I couldn't say, "Died."

"I know, Dear. He's gone home." As she touched my hand, I noticed the cross hanging around her neck. "Is there anything I can do?"

"Yes," I swallowed, "Is there anyway…uh…I could see him," I gulped, "… could I...I have a moment to say good-bye?"

"I'll see what I can do. Why don't you wait over there?" she pointed to a lone chair against the wall.

She waddled down the corridor.

About 20 minutes later she returned. "Let me take you to him."

She led me to a room where Josh lay on the narrow gurney, arms to his side, naked shoulders exposed from the white sheet that draped over him. In the otherwise dim room, a hooded light hanging above cast a bright glow over him wrapping him reverently like a large halo. He appeared as though he had been freshly scrubbed. His skin still glowed with the aliveness of a sleeping boy. His face remained remarkably unscarred. I touched his shoulder gently as though I was afraid with all his injuries I would hurt him. Hot tears burned as they rolled down my cheeks.

The minute I closed my eyes, the light came inside. I never had a dream while awake before, but I was having one then. I felt warm inside and out. Feeling a desert breeze blowing, as clearly as if I could touch him, Josh stood in front of me, smiling, dusty in his fatigues, his helmet tipped sideways, and leaning on his weapon that poked in the sand.

He spoke. "So, it's time to say good-bye, Old Buddy. But you're not to worry. Remember that time on the road to Kandahar? Now we're even. One thing, Old Buddy. You need to know and accept that things are preordained. I am leaving you a gift. You need to accept it. Treasure it." He smiled his crooked smile. "It's way cool up here. I have people to see and places to go. Gotta go now." He waved. "See to Jules, will ya? I'll always be watching over you, both of you. Love you."

The vision vaporized as I opened my eyes. Though something changed. The huge pain tightened around my heart had eased, lifted away like a drifting cloud, carrying with it a great part of the grief I felt. Though, there will always be the unfathomable sadness over his loss, this last goodbye was a miracle in my recovery from the pain and loss, as well as reconciling the residue of my combat experiences.

It's so stupid how you have to have some tragedy to open your heart and allow you to say all the things you feel for someone, but could never say in life. I sat down in the chair the nurse had provided for me and poured out all the feelings I had for Josh, all the fun we had growing up, all the times I had depended on him and he had carried me through.

"Love you too," I said as I stood. "Semper Fi," I saluted him.

The nurse was right. Josh had gone home.

Chapter 20

We're in Oregon – It Rains Sorrow

The plane ride as I accompanied the body of my friend back home, seemed interminable. My chest ached and I felt hollow inside.

"Sir, are you all right," the stewardess leaned across and set the glass of soda on my tray.

"I'll never be all right," I thought as I forearmed my wet face. I now knew what it felt like when someone says this kind of loss leaves a hole in your heart.

Shrouded in the Oregon mist, a contingent of Marines met our plane in Eugene, stood in formation four on each side and saluted as the coffin exited the plane onto the tarmac. As I stood saluting, standing at attention, the lump in my throat tightened. I felt light headed. The Marines carried the coffin to the Burnside's funeral van. Two Marines, wearing white gloves removed the flag by folding it in the standard triangular fold. It was loaded inside the van before the doors slammed shut. The van drove away, Josh's final ride home.

With a small group of friends and relatives surrounding her, Juliana stood hugging her arms around herself. After the deplaning ceremony, I was buried in hugs and tears from everyone.

Mom took a few steps forward and hugged me tight to her, a choked sob and gave me a quick kiss on my cheek. She leaned back, her face bathed in concern. "You okay, son?"

I nodded.

Don and Kelly, came over and stood in front of me. My throat swelled shut. No words would form. I reached out to my friend's parents. Kelly drew me close. "Please, Zack... come over as soon as you feel ...as often as... You're family, you know..."

"I know." I patted her back. "I know."

When I finally got to hold Jules, she leaned into my shoulder and sobbed. I threw my arms around her. "He loved you so much, Jules. So Much."

I wanted to be alone with Juliana, to just sit quietly, to tell her everything, and give her the medal. But that was not to be.

Shawna had backed off in deference to family then she slowly walked toward me. I had never seen her in person, though with modern technology, it wasn't the first time I had seen her. Before I knew it she jumped up and threw her arms around my neck. I buried my face in her long blond hair. It had been a long time since I'd caught a whiff anything that sweet.

We headed out through the airport and into the parking lot, my gear in one hand and the other holding Shawna's hand.

Mom smiled at us. "You sure look good in that uniform."

I smiled a crooked smile back, saddened as I remembered that I had worn my full dress blues because I knew they would have a ceremony as they removed the casket from the plane.

I loaded my duffle bag into the trunk of Mom's Chevy.

"You want to drive, Zack?" Mom asked.

"Naw, I just want to take in the sights. It's so good to be home."

"Good to have you here, too."

My thoughts scared me a little. I really did want to enjoy the scenery around me, didn't I? Was I apprehensive about driving? We'd see when I got into my own Wrangler.

The rain changed from mist to showers.

"Sit in front with Mom, Shawna. I'll stretch out in back." I opened the car door while I watched her slide her mini skirt across the seat. A very special pair of legs swung in under the dashboard.

I stood there continuing to take in the way she tucked in her skirt and feeling the rain on my face.

"Why don't you get in, you'll be soaked." Moms never change.

I held out my arms facing skyward. "Guess I just wanted to wash off a little Afghan dust," I said as I piled in back. "Never thought I'd be loving this rain. Sorry. I should have thought about getting your car all wet."

We took off. After we pulled onto Highway 126, Shawna hooked her arm over the front seat, reached over to hand me a manila envelope. I opened it. Out slid a bunch of letters and pictures her class made for me. Most of the ride home I spent opening the letters, reading them aloud, then she told me about each kid, their personalities and eccentricities. I laughed at her stories describing some of the antics teachers have to put up with. One kid had been fishing and brought the fish to school to show off. He ate it for lunch, carefully saving the bones, which he slipped into one of the prissiest girl's desk. The screaming, evidently, could be heard clear into the office. Eclipsing the somber scene from the airport wasn't easy, however Shawna and her class had done a pretty good job. It was good to laugh again.

When we came to the tunnel just before Mapleton I flinched and ducked.

"What was that?" Mom asked.

"Over there, whenever we approached a bridge we were always wary. You never knew when bombs or rocks or something worse could be thrown from bridges or high spots."

"I wondered about that," Shawna turned around again, hooking her elbow over the seat. "On our drive home with Snuzz, he ducked every time we went under a bridge."

"He was sure a good dog on that trip," Mom checked the rear view mirror. "He's very protective."

"Yeah," Shawna smiled revealing her set of beautiful straight white teeth as she glanced at Mom. "Remember that gas station where we stopped? We opened the window to get some air. That dog wouldn't let the attendant, anywhere near our car, growling, barking and baring his teeth."

Mom wheeled the car around a curve. "His name tag said, 'Jahid.' Jules said you had mentioned in one of your letters that Snuzz was very leery of Afghans. So somehow maybe Snuzz knew this guy was mid-eastern."

Shawna laughed. "Jahid paled. He looked as though he expected King Kong to jump from our car window. We just pumped our own gas."

"All that about Snuzz. So how is he, anyway?"

"You did a great job training him. I put him on a leash sometimes but he really obeys me. I take him to the beach often and let him run. I hope it was okay... I gave him some of Beast's tennis balls and..."

"I can hardly wait to see him. Hope he remembers me." I leaned back, my hands clasped behind my head, staring out the window.

"Well, he seems to think your room is his. I got him one of those big cushions. He snoozes on that while I watch TV, but he likes to sleep on your bed. You don't suppose it still has your scent, do you?"

I pictured Snuzz, the last time I saw him in the crate, sapphire blue eyes staring at me through the gate begging me not to let him go. Then I felt guilt like a shiver engulfing me so thoroughly that my heart ached. How could I sit here laughing, enjoying myself when there so many who would never come home? Josh would never get this chance.

Chapter 21
A Reunion

Driving to Shawna's place off of Munsel Creek Road provided a nice route to enjoy the scenic green surroundings of home. Oregon weather - where else is it raining one minute and clearing the next? The sun glinted off the bushes still strung with beads of rain as we pulled up in front of Shawna's white picket fence. White mounds of clouds tinged with purple drifted against the clear blue sky over the cottage.

"Wow! I didn't realize how much I missed the Oregon skies." I got out, stretched, taking in the beautiful crisp day then raced around to open Shawna's car door. With her mini skirt askew, Shawna swung out her slender gorgeous legs. As she stood rising to her full height of five foot four, I noticed that she was not only beautiful but also built. Shawna made my return have an unexpected spark.

She jumped up and kissed my cheek. I unhooked the gate. We walked to the door of the small bungalow hand in hand.

"Thanks for coming. It's really… uh…" I couldn't take my eyes off her large brown eyes that luminesced almost amber in the brilliant sunlight. I surprised myself as I slid my arms around her waist, lifted her and kissed her sweet soft lips. I let her down slowly our eyes absorbing each other.

"Think you'll remember where I live?"

"I don't think I'll have to Google Map Quest for this one. I'll call you…" I saluted her and backed away.

"You better."

I started back down the path. Glancing back, I caught her watching me over her shoulder as she unlocked the door.

"Okay, Mom. Let's go." I hopped in the front seat. "Snuzz awaits."

Was my heart beating this way, was I feeling anxious because I could hardly wait to see my dog, was it the remembrance of Shawna's warmth? Or was it something else?

"You like her a lot, huh? You know we got to know each other fairly well while we traveled cross-country to pick up Snuzz. I think she'd be a great..."

"I don't know her yet, Mom. Let's not start making any plans. But she is nice."

"Okay, okay. It's just that there hasn't been anyone since..."

We pulled into the driveway. "He's probably in the back yard. I guess he likes to watch things through the chain links."

She barely stopped and I had the door open, craning my neck to see where Snuzz was.

Mom pushed the garage door opener.

With that, Snuzz ducked out of his doghouse, shook himself off, stood by the gate, pawing the ground and wagging his whole backside never mind his tail. As he looked up, I remembered how his ears had personality as his head cocked to the side; one ear stood up with the tip bent over and the other bent down, then they were both at attention.

He recognized me when I got out. Spinners, he whirled around, his tail on super speed. Then he careened around the yard, leaping and twirling in the air.

"Come here, Snuzz. Come here, Boy," I called as I opened the gate. He sped toward me, hurtling into my arms knocking me off balance, twisting, wagging and licking my face as the two of us sprawled out on the ground rolling around. "Hey," I leaned away. " Don't lick my face off." I signaled, "Down."

Mom stood there laughing. "Yup. I can see he completely forgot you. I'll see you both inside," she said, opened the back door and disappeared inside.

I signaled again. "Roll over. Hey, Buddy, tummy rub?" We wrestled around a few more minutes. Then Snuzz stood up shook himself off. Up on two feet, he danced for a second then like a bullet he raced around the yard a couple of times before he came back and sat at my feet.

I wasn't sure my uniform would ever be the same again, wet dog hairs and grass clinging here and there. I brushed myself off glad that most of Florence developed on a bed of sand dunes so when it rained there wasn't mud to clean off.

That night was heaven. I was in my own bed, a tad roomier than my rack, with Snuzz curled up against to me. "We're home Snuzz, we're home." I buried my head in his fur.

Chapter 22

A Somber Day

I awoke the morning of the funeral, the rain beating against the window. Lying in the room where I grew up, the one I shared so much with Josh; I knew as soon as I could I would need to leave, to find my own way. Though how could I ask Mom not to turn this room into an art room? I wanted to be able to come back here whenever I wanted to find the memories. Half the pictures lining the walls included Josh.

I stood in the shower luxuriating in the hot water. Couldn't seem to get enough of a genuine hot shower. While I donned my dress blues, I recalled some of the times we had been dressed up like this and gone places together, how proud we were to be Marines in our dress blues.

As we entered the lobby of the funeral home, the fragrance along with the beauty of the floral sprays softened the somber scene. The rainy bleak day mirrored all my visions of the darkness that filled me as we made our way into Burnside chapel for the service. We sat down in the seats designated for family. My mom patted my knee with a hand clenched around a wad of Kleenex. I held Jules close to me as though I could shelter her from the sorrow that engulfed us. I was so grateful to be surrounded by those who were truly my family. It meant I could take care of Juliana, though when I caught sight of Shawna, I felt regret that I hadn't thought to invite her to sit with me.

Jules and her parents had never been close. They sat coolly on the other side of her, their demeanor almost fearful of connecting.

A crooked smile slipped across my face as I remembered that I had once prepared a special speech for the wedding, the notes that I crumpled and couldn't deliver. I wondered, could I stand up there today, in back of the lectern, facing all those mourners and say what I wanted to say? I took the notes out of my pocket, fumbling around with them, trying to get the 3'by 5' cards in order. I glanced over at Jules, ran a hand across my crew cut, with my eyebrows raised.

Jules squeezed my hand. "Yes, you can."

"You could always read my mind."

Don rose from his seat slowly and ambled up to the dais. Facing the audience, he cleared his throat and began to speak about his son. Behind him pictures of Josh flashed on the screen while Don related stories about the giggling little rascal Joshua had been as a toddler. He reminisced about Cub Scouts, little league, fishing trips, rebuilding that Mustang, watching him play football, and I was right there with him in all those good times. There weren't many dry eyes, especially not those of his mom, Kelly.

I glimpsed Jules as Don related stories that included Jules, wearing a choked smile as the tears rolled down her cheeks. Our lives were so intertwined.

Then it was my turn. I grabbed my cards from the pew and pulled at the neck of my uniform. My heart pounded as I approached the podium and adjusted the note cards in front of me. I took several deep breaths. I knew it was all a stall, but I just needed to swallow a few times, lose the lump and get my head together. I glanced out at the range of people who filled the chapel. The men in their dress blues stood out among the friends from church, high school together with college teammates, neighbors, friends and relatives. I gazed up at the ceiling, "I hope you're looking down here, Joshua Cole. There are a whole lot of people here who love you."

I adjusted the mike upward. "We came to say good-bye Old Buddy." I paused for a moment and recalled. "I remember the first time you called me Old Buddy. It was our opening game of the season and our first season on varsity. Within ten minutes, you had thrown two fantastic passes. I caught each one just short and stepped over into the end zone. As the game progressed, we were behind two points. One minute before the end of the fourth quarter, you threw me another long pass and with a five-yard charge, we won. They carried me off the field though it should have been you. As we came into the locker room, you hung your arm around my neck, practically choking me as you spoke, 'Well, we did it Old Buddy! What a team we make.' And what a team we did make."

"How lucky I was to have you as my best buddy, my brother, as you shared your family with me. Remember the shaving cream fight we had after you asked your dad to show us how to shave, 'real quick'? Real quick. HA! HA! After a few cuts and scrapes during an hour's worth of time, we were chasing each other down the hall squirting the shaving cream all over each other. There your Mom stood with her hands on her hips, laughing at all the little bloody pieces of toilet paper stuck here and there to our cut up faces."

After several stories about the service pranks in the barracks plus his bravery on our Afghan tour, I finished off with the one where we arrived home after a fishing trip. The two of us chased Jules around her front yard with our catch, fish guts drizzling out and all.

I stood for a moment in silence. If I finished relating all our stories, then I would have to face the one simple fact. There would be no more stories. I gulped, the lump swelling again in my throat. "I will carry the lessons we learned together with me all my life. I wouldn't be here today, if it wasn't for you... I owe you... my life... Good-bye, Old Buddy..." I turned toward the open casket, encasing a sleeping Marine in full dress and saluted. "Semper Fi."

The burial was quiet with just family. I remember the cars crawling up the road encased in giant spruce trees while rain streamed between the windshield wipers. But I can't remember what anyone said at the gravesite as we stood there beneath the sky full of tears raining down on us. My heart was beating out of chest, though not loud enough to drown out the sobs from Jules and Kelly. I held it together until Jules laid the white rose on the casket, scooped up a handful of dirt then dropped it in on top of the casket with a crumbling thud. Was that rain or tears streaming down my face and dripping off my lips? I licked away the salty residue.

This was so final. I wanted to scream but no sounds would come out.

At the wake, sad Christmas decorations that hung throughout Josh's parent's home seemed to intensify the grief. The rain had lapsed into fog adding another layer of gloom. I sauntered out back sitting at the picnic table under a tree, visualizing Josh and I rope climbing or doing some of the training exercises we had devised before reporting for duty. The tree house we built still clung to the big spruce. Jules joined me and we sat for a long time.

Drifting from the neighboring house, Christmas carols interrupted our silence. Jules looked up. "I'm remembering how your mom used to take us Christmas caroling."

"The last time!" I laughed. "When Brandon heard us outside his house, he streaked, naked, past his picture window."

"You would think of that…I just remembered Josh, standing there, his stocking cap pulled down with that silly red and green scarf around his neck, singing at the top of his lungs…so off key…" She wiped her eyes "How are we going to live without him, Zack, how?"

There could be no answer to that question.

Somehow the wake ended. I stayed around helping Kelly and Don straighten and clean up the kitchen. It was kind of Shawna to stay to help out too.

Shawna and I drove up to Cape Perpetua Point. I didn't feel like talking. Shawna didn't push it. For a long while, we just sat viewing the expansive Pacific. The sun hid itself behind purple storm clouds while beams streaked through the casting silver spots on the water, like the rays from heaven.

"Isn't that spectacular?" Shawna leaned against me.

"He's reaching down, saying good bye," I laid my hand on hers.

Chapter 23

A Luncheon Date

In downtown Florence on Bay Street, Shawna and I sat by the window in the Restobar, I always felt more comfortable sitting with my back to a wall where I could see the whole room. Couples sat at the bar and two other tables in the cozy restaurant.

As the sun streamed though the paned window, I stared out at the Siuslaw River watching a fishing boat head out under the bridge. When Jules came sauntering by concentrating on the sidewalk in front of her, I knocked on the window gesturing for her to come in.

She paused a moment on the brick stairs then came through the door.

"We just ordered burgers, why don't you join us?"

"I...couldn't really... just wanted to say, 'Hi.'" She flashed a quick sad smile, still hanging onto the door.

"Sure you could." I hopped up quickly and took her hand off the door then turned toward the waitress. "Give us another burger and a Coke." Leading her, I pulled a chair over from another table, and patted the seat as I glanced around the room. What was I expecting? I didn't know why, but always being vigilant seemed to be a curse I couldn't lose even in the safety of Florence. I thought of the cliché, "Old habits die hard."

"Well...Okay."

"So how have you been doing?" Shawna asked.

Jules looked through the window. "Doing, I guess."

"If you'll excuse me." Shawna pointed as she got up, waved

and headed toward the restroom.

"So much to do arranging everything, and filling out paper work. I've been quite busy."

"You need any help?" I reached for her hand.

"No, Don and Kelly have been really helpful. It's all done. Sometimes I …" she folded her hands.

"Yeah, a task like that," I paused, "having it all finished instantly says, 'this is final.'"

I thumbed a tear from her cheek.

I reached for her then held both her hands in mine.

"That's what it is, Zack. It's so final."

"I know." I rolled her hand in mine seeing the sun glint off the diamonds in her wedding band.

Shawna sat down just as the hamburgers were set in front of us. Since being home, I still couldn't get used to the portions of food served. "I forgot how huge these burgers were." I took a monster bite before a guilty thought ran to the poverty I'd seen in Afghanistan.

"I don't think I'm hungry," Jules dabbed at her eyes.

"Sure you are." I noticed a little shiny oozing at the side of Jules' burger. It reminded me of a time in elementary school. "I just recalled something that should really peak your appetite. Remember that time I put snails in all the girls' lunches?"

"That's supposed to make me feel like eating?"

"No, but you're smiling."

"Well, I'm hungry." Shawna said crunching a potato chip.

"The teacher was so mad. Did she ever find out you were the culprit?" Absently Jules took a bite of her burger.

"No one told, but she must've been able to tell by the huge grin on my face. You're smiling. And see, I got you to take a bite."

"That's just because I remembered how I got you back…" Jules took another bite, "by having you over for lunch and making your 'tuna sandwich' out of Tabby's cat food."

"It's not polite to talk with your mouth full." I wiped her face.

We laughed.

"Hey, we were going to the show why don't come with us?"

"I wouldn't want to intrude."

"Nonsense." I turned toward Shawna. "You don't mind, do you?"

"Uh…no…sure why don't you come too?"

"The Karate Kid is playing. It's supposed to be pretty good." I said as we gathered up our stuff. I paid the bill and we exited the restaurant.

"Meet us there, okay." I couldn't be sure Jules would come to the theater, but I knew it'd do her good.

Minutes later we were in the parking lot. I was so glad to see Jules pull in behind us.

I stepped up to the counter paying for the tickets. "You want to share a large popcorn?"

"Sure," the girls agreed.

"A large popcorn and Pepsis all around."

The boy shoveled in the popcorn.

"Lot's of butter, please."

He leaned on the butter squirter.

"Oh, no, I don't like butter," Shawna said.

The owner shoved the already buttered popcorn across the counter.

"Sorry. I know Jules really loves her butter."

We had our choice of seats. Afternoon shows are interesting in Florence. I glanced around. There were about six other people in the theater all with white hair. Shawna called them Q-Tips.

I sat in the middle of my two favorite women feeling a bit guilty that Shawna didn't eat much of the popcorn, though Jules and I did – with much gusto.

The last scene over with the credits scrolling down found us walking out. I left the theater shaking my head. "How did that kid get in such great shape? I think he could have wiped the mat with my martial arts instructor!"

Seeing Jules smiling set us all smiling.

"Thanks, I think I needed that. I haven't eaten this much all week. Now I've stuffed myself." Jules rubbed her stomach. "I'll be remembering this tomorrow with all those hulls stuck in my teeth."

After I went to bed that evening, I woke in the middle of the night snapping straight up in bed. Overhead thunder boomed as lightening lit the room. I threw myself over Snuzz whose eyes told me he felt exactly like the way I felt, the two of us yoked in fear. Lying there I recalled times when we had to react instantly to sounds like that while knowing exactly what the sounds had indicated. It simulated a nightmare while I was awake. I had nearly forgotten or conveniently buried the memory of seeing one of our platoon members stepping solidly on an IED. I squeezed my eyes shut trying to block out the memory of a brother being blasted to pieces, leaving me wondering. "Why wasn't it me," I pounded my pillow. "Couldn't I have done something?"

Snuzz laid his head on my chest. I ruffled his fur. Sweating, I tossed and turned until finally dropping off to sleep, Snuzz and me.

Chapter 24

Facing the Day

When the next morning dawned crisp, clear though cold, I was glad I had called Jules the night before and asked her to drive with me to Driftwood Shores to the beach where the three of us had spent our summers romping on the sand.

I patted the seat for Snuzz to join me in the Jeep. I would miss having Snuzz and my Jeep when my leave ended.

Snuzz paced back and forth in the back seat, wagging and panting with his tongue hanging out. When we got to Jules' place off 15th Street, I expected her to dash right out as she used to in the old days. When she didn't, I walked up the stone path to the door, opened the rickety screen and knocked.

No answer.

"Jules. It's me, Zack. Are you ready?" I rang the bell, but no answer. I pounded the door. When I tried the handle, the door was locked. I circled around to the side and peered through the bedroom window. Jules lay there still there huddled under the covers.

"Jules." I called out.

"Go away."

"Are you all right?"

"Go away, Zack."

"I'm coming in." I went to the back door. It was unlocked so I let myself in, dashed through the kitchen racing down the hallway to her room.

I sat down on the bed. "Are you sick? Are you okay?"

When she didn't answer. I pulled the covers back. Her face

was red and puffy with swollen eyes. I bent down and kissed her forehead. "Just a minute. I'll be right back. I know just what you need."

I rushed out the front door to the jeep and let Snuzz out. As if on cue, he bounded down, straight up the path, into the house where I'd left the front door ajar. The tired screen door hung open leaving Snuzz just enough space. He snaked around the screen door. With me right behind, he disappeared through the hall then leaped on the bed with Jules. He knew what to do. And he did it in own inimitable way. By the time I got there, he was leaning over her, licking her face. He grabbed the edge of the quilt in his teeth, tugging it away from her. Snuzzing under her hands until her arms were around him, he curled up there quietly in her arms.

"I'll be back in a minute." I went off into the kitchen. The counters were strewn with dirty dishes, cereal boxes and empty soup cans. I rinsed the dishes and threw them in the dishwasher before scrounging around getting the last three eggs in the fridge. I whipped up some scrambled eggs and toast. "Breakfast is almost ready so you better get some clothes on," I hollered.

When I went back to get her, she was zipping up her jeans. I turned away while she threw on her tee shirt. "Better put on some tennis shoes, too. We're going to the beach."

Like being dragged by the back of her collar, she entered the kitchen then slumped into the chair.

I set the plate down in front of her. I rounded the table and sat across the table from her. "Want some milk and sugar in your coffee?"

She nodded. I reached over and fixed it for her while she held her head in her hands.

She pushed a few bites around her plate.

"Eat. You don't want me to feed you like that time at lunch in the cafeteria when I fed you that banana."

"Fed? Huh! I had more banana up my nose than in my mouth." She smiled then swallowed a few bites.

"I know..." I toyed with a bite of eggs on my fork. "Right now, eating is like a mouthful of food is being shoved through a straw. I felt that way all week. In the end Mom's cooking got the better of my resistance." We ate without saying much. "You know. I haven't been able to sleep in my old room. He's there too. I had a thought yesterday when I came home from the movies. I am going to take comfort in the fact that so much of the room is filled with shared memories, that he still surrounds me with his friendship."

I reached down and gave Snuzz a piece of toast.

The corners of Jules mouth curled. Then she fed Snuzz an egg bite. "Maybe I'll sleep in one of his shirts tonight."

"There you go." I drank my last slurp of coffee. "Come on. Let's take a ride. I'll come back later and do the dishes." I took her hand leading her out, Snuzz tagging along behind us. "Grab your coat. It'll be cold at the beach."

"Thanks. What are you now, my dad?" She shoved me through the door into the sunshine.

Chapter 25

A Revelation at the Beach

I opened the door of the Jeep. Snuzz popped into the passenger seat. I pointed. Eying me for a moment, he stuck his tail between his legs and lumbered into the back.

"Come on now, Snuzz, you didn't think that was your permanent seat." With that he turned facing front and shoved his head between the two front seats, like, "There, I'll show you."

After Jules scooted into the Jeep, we drove in silence until we were well out on Rhododendron Drive, well, almost silence, with nothing but Snuzz panting over our shoulders. Soon the memories started flowing. The times we double dated, the after football game parties. We went way back to the mud football games with the girls in the neighborhood.

"I was just thinking about that party Michael Gessler had," Jules leaned against the window.

"The one where we went on that stupid treasure hunt?" I said.

"We went door to door asking for stuff like a jingle bell, a rubber band, cheese, a feather, and even a pair of panty hose with a run. Speaking of cheese, remember that awful smelling Limburger cheese we got that I stashed it in your pocket?" Jules smiled up at me.

"Geez, did that ever smell up my coat! PU. It smelled so bad I had to leave the jacket outside. Could you believe that girl actually gave us a pair of her bikini underwear?"

"I was so embarrassed when Josh started running all over with the pink bikinis on his head," Jules rolled her eyes.

"We won too. We were back 10 minutes before everyone

else and we were the only team who got everything on their list."

"Getting bored waiting for the party to come back, I think it was your idea to break off bits of that horrible smelling cheese and hide them around Michael's room."

Before we knew it our sad memories turned to laughter. The more we laughed, the more Snuzz howled.

We headed into the gravel parking space just before Driftwood Shores. After I put on my stocking cap, I found another cap lodged in the seat. I pulled it on her head down over her eyes. "There," I patted her head. "Wouldn't want you to catch cold."

She rolled up the edge." Gee, thanks, Dad."

After we donned our heavy coats, we sprinted to the sand, hand in hand with Snuzz right beside us. We didn't stop until we hit the flat stretch of sand glazed by the withdrawing tide. Our breath streamed out in puffs. After the run, the lack of wind and the brilliant sun made us believe it was warmer than 40 degrees.

Snuzz sprinted about in dog nirvana, prancing at the waves and scampering back when a wave chased him. He took a taste of the water then shook himself off. "Except that Mom told me she walked him here, you'd think he had ever seen the ocean before."

I picked up a stick with Snuzz leaping after it. I hurled the stick ahead on the beach. Snuzz had it back in seconds.

"Boy, he's fast." Jules pushed a strand of hair under her cap.

"He was something over there." I told her about the time he took down the Taliban in the alley. "You should have seen that guy's face with Snuzz on his jugular."

"So Snuzz wasn't just a pet over there?"

"He was absolutely a member of our team." While I kept throwing the stick for Snuzz, I went on to explain some of the tasks I trained Snuzz to do.

"Let me." She grabbed the stick and threw it.

"You throw like a girl."

"Yeah and that's bad?"

"Well," I hooked my arm around her neck. "I guess it's kinda cute."

With my arm around her, we sauntered back toward a huge log that had washed up on the shore.

"Ew…My hands are freezing." She withdrew her hands from her pocket and rubbed them together.

I put my hands around hers blowing on them.

It was the first time in all our years of friendship and closeness, that her touch took my breath away. I dropped her hands with a wave of guilt washing over me.

"Come on." I hooked my arm in hers and stepped up the pace.

I pointed to a log.

"Race you there." She took off running.

Snuzz took off after her when he noticed a couple of other dogs chasing each other. I tensed at first, recalling how protective he became over there with the wild packs of dogs. But he seemed to sense these were playful pups. I liked seeing him romping with the other dogs. This wasn't anything he'd been able to do in Afghanistan.

I caught up with Jules and plopped down straddling the log. Snuzz was way ahead when he noticed we had stopped. He spun, kicking up sand and raced back to the log. He sat there panting with his tongue hanging out. I signaled him to lie down.

Jules tossed her leg over and sat facing me. Before I could pull out the medal, before I could tell her all the things I had wanted to say, she said, "I have something to tell you." Tears welled in her eyes.

Her face seemed so very serious. What could be wrong now? My heart was beating loud enough for it to scare the rest of the dogs on the beach.

I waited.

She pulled her hands out of her pocket and staring down at the sandy pile of seaweed.

"I'm listening."

She concentrated on her hands while she traced a bark strip with her finger. She tipped her face up and bore her soft green eyes into mine. "Josh and I are having a baby."

I didn't know how to feel but when we both broke into a grin, we knew that we both had been given a gift.

All at once we were in each other's arms and my lips brushed hers, I drew away with just a hint of a kiss. When the delicious warmth of her drew away, I decided that I couldn't let that happen again.

She needed to know about Josh's last night, so I told her about the accident. That's where I started. Having told no one else about my vision, but with news of their child, I shared it with her, I knew this must be the gift Josh had told me about. I would, as he asked, always treasure this child as if it was mine.

"Josh will be with us forever," I managed to say. With that I pressed the St. Christopher's metal in her hand. I told her all the times Josh had spoken of her, shared some of her letters, of the happiness he experienced because of her and of his last words.

I wiped a tear dripping from her chin.

After some long moments of silence, I said, "We better go."

We didn't say much on the way home, a few more memories followed by an awkward silence.

As she eased out of the car, I said, "I'm sorry. I..."

"Nothing to be sorry for." She ran into the house.

That night the nightmares began. I could smell it. I could taste it. I could feel the desert sands pitting my face and I was there, facing the man with an explosive device strapped to his chest. Frantically I pulled at the wires girding the man, but the timer kept ticking, affecting me like lemon juice dripping in a wound. Horror covered the wife's face as she shielded her son. As though it was slow motion movie, I ran. The man shrieked an ungodly shriek or was it me screaming?

The explosion blasted me through the air. I sat up, shaking my head and rubbing my eyes. Trying to quiet my heart rate, I laid back down afraid to close my eyes.

Snuzz curled next to me. I hugged him close as I heard the knock on the door.

"Everything okay in there?"

"Sure, Mom, everything is okay. Go back to bed."

Chapter 26

Church

The next day was Sunday. Other than the wake service, I hadn't been to church for a very long time. The last being a time when Josh was with us. After my restless night, I needed to feel that sense of calm. Maybe I'd find it there. I knew we'd have to break the barrier doing some of the things we'd all done together. Jules and I might as well do it now when we needed it the most. I got up early to call her. "Be ready in a half an hour."

"Ready?"

I heard her yawn.

"I thought it was time I went to church. Knew you'd want to be there too."

"Come on, Zack. I..."

"Be ready, I'm coming. I'm on my way." I hung up listening to her protests die away.

As I drove up I could see her pull the curtain back, then she met me at the door with her one hand on her hip, holding a glass of clear bubbly liquid in the other.

"You look awful?" I stuck my hands in my pockets.

"Thanks a lot. I'd like to see what you'd look like after a bout with morning sickness."

I pulled the screen door open, only to find that it was no longer attached to the jamb. It thudded on the porch held up only with my hand. I laid it against the gray siding and walked in.

Holding Jules at arms distance, I searched her pale face. "Are you okay?"

"Yeah. It usually stops about now if I eat some crackers accompanied by 7UP." She raised her glass.

"Church'd do you good, if you're feeling up to it."

"I know. I'm okay. Wait a minute. I'll get a skirt on."

I called Shawna but she had already taken off for church.

The color was coming back to Jules' face when she returned. She twisted her dark waves up and pinched them together with one of those hair clamps. I usually didn't like when girls twisted their hair up with hunks sticking out, but Jules hair looked damned good that way.

"I did what I said," Jules said.

"Which was what?"

"It helped. I mean wearing Josh's shirt. I dreamt he was right there with his arms around me."

"He's coming with us today, too." I took her hand as we walked to the Jeep.

Upon entering the church, we were greeted by several members.

"Good to see you back, Zack," Ken, greeted me with his hardy handshake. He held on for a moment with both hands. Without saying anything, he stared into my eyes communicating his empathy and concern.

"Juliana, Dear, how are you doing?" Suzanne asked, her face wearing a sympathetic smile, as she hugged Jules for a long while, rubbing her back. "Let me know if I can do anything."

Jules nodded.

I scanned the area around me checking for what I wasn't sure until I saw Shawna down the center aisle, so we scooted in the pew beside her. I smiled when the small boy at the end of the pew took out his Hot Wheels car running it up and down his leg.

The Christian church always rocks with great music, enough to raise anyone's spirit. I usually enjoyed watching the screen up front and singing along with the music. Today the lump in my throat silenced me.

I noticed that Jules wasn't singing either.

How did I know that especially today, Jules and I needed to be here at this very Sunday service? The title of the service was, *Dealing with Loss*. There were a few moments when I caught Jules wiping her eyes. On the whole we both felt better for having been there, with her leaning against me for support.

The Shawna walked with Jules and I as we greeted friends in the lobby. Out to the dirt parking lot, I invited my two girls to breakfast.

"No, you two go on without me intruding." Jules said.

"Nonsense, you are not intruding. Huh, Shawna?"

"Yes... uh, I mean no, you aren't... intruding, I mean."

"Okay, Shawna. Meet us at the Little Brown Hen. Nothing but comfort food there!"

After a stint in Afghanistan, gorging myself on the huge portions of food back here at home was sheer heaven. The Little Brown Hen was certainly the place to do it. I lit into my side of biscuits with gravy then finished off my pancakes, fried eggs and sausage. All I remember about that meal was how great over easy eggs tasted as opposed to scrambled powdered eggs, though I still felt a measure of guilt over my enjoyment.

"How's that yogurt and cereal, Shawna?" I said shoveling in my last sausage whole.

After Shawna daintily tasted her dry toast, she said, "Don't know how you can eat so much of that gravy."

"Remember Jules? You once invited Josh and me for breakfast. You made your forever-to-be-forgotten biscuits and gravy. You could stand your fork up in the gravy or play hockey with the biscuit. I didn't eat much that day."

Jules rolled her eyes.

Just then a little girl came skipping in beside her mother. A rhinestone jeweled tiara bounced on her blonde curly hair.

"Say, Jules, didn't you have a crown like that when you were little?"

"I don't like to think about the last time I wore it."

Shawna held her toast out. "I had a tiara like that..."

"Oh I remember. We were doing a play. Your mom told us not to light the candles," I said.

"I would have died if it wasn't for you." Jules' brow furrowed.

"Yeah. You say that now but, boy, you were so mad when I tackled you to the ground and rolled you over and over. Your princess outfit was still smoking when I doused you with the hose."

"Yes, I guess I did blow my stack until I realized if you hadn't come around the corner when you did..."

A sudden dish crashed to the floor in the kitchen. I jumped and threw myself over Jules. When I realized how ridiculous that reaction was, I stood. "Guess it's time to go, girls."

"Yeah, I guess so!" Shawna stood and straightened out her sweater.

"See Ya." I waved to Shawna on her way to her car.

Quiet prevailed on the way to take Jules home.

"Did you realize you barely said a word to Shawna all during breakfast?"

"Huh? I didn't. It's just that you and I had so many things to talk about. Do you think she noticed?" I peered straight ahead as I rubbed my hand back and forth across my crew cut.

"Oh, she noticed all right."

Chapter 27

Fix It up

Jules ambled into her house while I walked back to my Jeep, got the tool kit, set it on the stairs. I started hammering some of the molding back onto the screen door.

"What's all this racket?" Jules asked as she came back to the door.

"What's it look like?" I kept on hammering.

"Well, God knows I needed to have that front door fixed. This place is falling apart. Josh and I had such big plans to turn this place into our dream cottage." She scrutinized the porch stairs, slats missing with the paint peeling. She gave the rickety railing a shake. "I don't think it's supposed to be so springy."

"I guess we can't slide down that one like we used to do on the banister in Josh's place." I lifted the screen door in place. "Could you hold it steady while I screw the new hinges into the door jamb."

As she reached up to hold the screen door, I noticed the tear dripping off her chin. "Hey, I'm sorry."

"You're always saying you're sorry when there's nothing to be sorry for."

I screwed in the last hinge.

"You want to come in for a cup of coffee."

I followed her through the living room noticing that her once immaculate house was strewn with clothes. Dirty dishes sat here and there.

"I'll be right there." I heard her rustling around in the kitchen while I gathered up some of the clutter in the living room and dining room. I straightened up as I went along. Maybe I'm away from the base, but the sense of order the service gave me remained embedded in my psyche.

In the kitchen, I saw that nothing was cleaned up from the other day when I made breakfast.

"Don't worry about all this stuff. I'll get to it."

"I promised I'd come back to do the dishes but I left you with a mess…" I rinsed the dishes and loaded them into the dishwasher.

"You don't have to do that, " she said as she shoved a cereal box into the cupboard.

"I insist."

"Thanks, I haven't cared about much lately. Though seeing the counter cleaned up does feel better." She slugged my shoulder. "Besides, my sister and my niece are coming to stay with me next week. I have to run my bulldozer through here."

"I'm glad they're coming to be here with you."

"I'll be better when I get back to work next week. Teaching pretty much fills my brain from the first bell to the last."

Jules set the table with cups and spoons. I got out the sugar and milk. She heaped a teaspoonful of sugar into her half a cup, then poured milk to fill it to the brim.

"So I see you still like it the way your mother fixed it for us on cold days."

"That was a long time ago. Remember…on rainy days, that old blanket we draped over the backs of those leather chairs in my den?" She re-clipped her hair on top of her head.

"Do you remember the password for our secret club?"

I took a sip of my coffee while I searched my mind but couldn't remember."

"Za-Jo-Ju, how could you forget?"

"Ah, yes, remember? We pretended it meant, 'Way cool,' in Japanese. But it was just the first two letters of all our names..." I stopped speaking.

Silence prevailed for a long moment. She turned away, her

eyes red and glassy.

I took a drink, not wanting to make her cry any more.

"Hey," Jules covered my hand with hers. "All of these memories are so wonderful. Though they're bitter thoughts at this moment, they still bring sweetness along with the sorrow."

She wiped her cheek. "Our recollections are like a treasure chest filled with gems, glimpses of wonder, that bring him back to us even though it's only for a moment." She sniffled as she peered straight into my eyes. "Promise me, we will always share these stories without tip-toeing around trying to avoid the subject because of being afraid I'll fall apart."

"Yeah, I suppose that would be like letting him fade away. The stories keep him alive." I held both her hands.

"He's still with us."

We studied each other as both our eyes brimmed.

Chapter 28

Nights Are Too Long

That night, after a couple of beers, or maybe more, I wasn't counting I closed the door to my room leaving Snuzz in the hallway. Somehow his presence brought a wave of guilt over me. I lay down stretched out on my bed, hands behind my head while I glanced around my room. All the pictures, trophies and banners reminded me of Josh. I wondered how Jules could do it – stay there in her house where everything there must remind her of Josh. When I walked through their living room this afternoon, I visualized picking that sofa up at a garage sale. Josh and I maneuvered it through the front door then dragged it around the room to three or four locations until Jules had decided where it fit best. Finally she said, "No, I think it looks better back over there..." the exact place where we first placed it.

Snuzz scratched on the door, which immediately brought me out of my melancholy mood.

"Okay, Boy. Just relax. I'll see you in the morning." I rolled over and went to sleep.

Suddenly bombs exploded all around me. Fires leapt on all sides. I ran and ran as fast I as I could, fingers of flames lapping at my legs, machine gun fire flinging up blasts of sand. The enemy advanced, coming closer and closer. The smell of smoke and dust filled my lungs, I couldn't breathe. I clawed my way up the sandy terrain, bullets whizzing past my ears.

Not knowing how I got there, I ducked down in the Humvee with the bullets pinging off the fender. Dust whirled around the

Humvee. I coughed. I gasped for air.

Blood dripped from my hands to my wrists down my arms to my lap. "Hayworth!" the red flow spurted from Hayworth's neck. I wrapped my hand around the wound. Red oozed through my fingers. I couldn't stop it. I screamed. "It's okay. You'll be okay."

"Mama," rang over and over in my ears. I thrashed around covering my ears. "Make it stop!" I sat up in a sweat. I shook my head as though I could make the images disappear.

"Zack, are you all right?" My mom stood by my bed.

Snuzz crawled in my lap.

"I'm fine. Go back to bed. I'm okay. And why'd you let the dog back in? Get him out of here!" I shoved Snuzz to the floor.

As I was lying back down, Mom pulled the covers up around my chin and kissed me on the forehead.

I grabbed the blanket and rolled over. "Geez, Mom, just go! Leave me alone! Go back to bed!"

Chapter 29

Afterward

At about eleven thirty the next morning, I came into the kitchen and headed for the refrigerator. I grabbed a beer listening as I popped the top.

"Isn't it a bit early for beer." Mom sipped her coffee and turned the newspaper over.

"Lay off," I gulped down a couple swigs.

"You want breakfast?"

"I'm drinking it." I reached for a couple more Coors then charged back to my room. I slammed the door behind me, closing Snuzz in the hallway.

After a few more beers, the memory of the dream filled my thoughts, somber like the aftermath of an IED explosion. Anger seized me like a vise. I raked my arm across the top of my bureau knocking the pictures with a trophy onto the floor. I screamed. Shattered glass littered the carpet.

I started down the hall toward the kitchen.

Mom met me half way. "What was that?"

"It was nothing, Mom, nothing at all."

"Well, it must have been something," she said as she watched me grab the broom and dustpan out of the closet.

She reached for the broom.

I grabbed it back. "I'll get it. I just knocked over a picture."

"Let me help you." She followed me down the hall.

I stopped cold. "I told you, Mom. I got it! Okay?"

I swept up the glass dumping the shards into the metal

wastebasket with a crash.

While I replaced the stuff on the bureau, I heard the scratching on the door. "Oh, Snuzz, I forgot about you." I opened the door. He bounded in sniffing, checking out the broom and the dustpan, circled back to sit on my foot.

I spent the afternoon looking on the net for jobs. How do they expect someone to get experience when all the jobs call for previous experience? I chugged the rest of my beer down. Then I remembered. Shawna. After the funeral, we had talked about doing a picnic while enjoying the sunset again. I told I'd pick her up, drive up to Cape Perpetua, where we'd eat and watch the sun sizzle into the ocean. It was a spot where I might be able to get my head together.

I stood in the shower for a long time letting the ice-cold spray of water flood down the top of my head to wake me up, then luxuriated in the warm sting of the hot water full force on my back and my head. After I shaved, I felt better. I threw on my sweatshirt over my Levis.

"See ya later," I called back as I headed out toward the Jeep.

I lowered the top. I was glad I had. After downing those beers, I needed the brace of the brisk wind in my face. I stopped at Freddie's for a few of bottles of wine before heading to Shawna's place.

Shawna must've been watching out her window. Her door popped open and she looked spectacular. I appreciated the sway of her hips as she ambled to the car, her plaid mini skirt swaying back and forth over her black tights, the picnic basket swinging by her side.

"Would you mind putting the top up?" She flipped her bangs aside then patted her hair.

"I guess winter isn't the best time for the top down, especially when your hair looks so good."

After I raised the top, we were off. The clouds moved in, coloring the blue sky with whites and grays. By the time we climbed the road up to Cape Perpetua, my stomach rumbled. I hadn't eaten all day. My head pulsated in pain.

Shawna reached for the basket in the back seat. "We have veggie sandwiches, lettuce, tomatoes sprouts, avocado on multigrain. Here, try the potato salad I made."

"Uh, very…uh...healthy," I said thinking how fried chicken, like Jules always fixed, would've hit the spot. I picked up a bottle of wine, uncorked it, handed her a paper cup and poured.

"To the sunset," she touched my cup then tipped it to the sunset. By then the skies were brilliant golden shades turning peach with purple clouds billowing among the rays, all the palette of colors glazing the ocean.

"To the sunset." I toasted the sky then downed my wine, adding several more to the tally.

"Sure you don't want any more?" I poured myself another.

When the food was gone, I slipped my arm around her drawing her close. When she tilted her face up, I kissed her, just as the sun sizzled into the horizon.

"Want to go to my house?" Shawna said in a breathy voice that promised a lot.

"Sounds good to me."

Chapter 30

Promises, Promises

With Shawna riding shotgun, we started back down the winding curves of 101 toward Florence. I sped up enjoying the rush from taking the S-curves in the road at 50 mph or more. I had never been a speed freak before. At that moment, though, I was really into it.

"Hey, Zack! Slow it down!"

"Why? Sit back. Relax."

"I mean it, Zack," she said bracing her arms with hands against the dash. "This is dangerous!" She gazed glassy-eyed over the edge down about a hundred feet to the ocean as her voice escalated. "It's a long way down there. Now please, slow down!"

I had to bite my tongue to keep from yelling at her, "Leave me alone!"

"Okay, okay," I said as I let off the gas and applied the brake, maybe just in time. We swerved, spun, and skidded into the rough gravel at the edge of the road while Shawna screamed and grabbed her chest. My driving skills, or lack thereof, gave us a mighty close look at the shear drop off. Listening to my heart beating on super speed, I guess we were both hyperventilating for a minute. There weren't many words spoken.

"I'm sorry," I finally managed to say as I reached for her hand and squeezed. However, was I really sorry? That was as high as I'd been since the school incident in Afghanistan or when I drove the Humvee backwards.

I watched my speed the rest of the way back.

I hadn't been inside Shawna's house before. I had to admire a young woman who bought her own place. Her dad spent time helping her fix up the older house. As I stepped in, I glanced around the room. "Wow!" It resembled a dollhouse. From the lacy curtains to antique satin settee to the mahogany end tables draped in those little doily things, it reminded me of the little museum in town. I rotated my head around taking in all the old photos that hung on the walls with pink and green ribbon.

"You like? My grandmother gave me all these old pictures."

That's what it reminded me of, Gran's house.

"Sit down. I'll get a couple of glasses."

I set the bottles of wine on the coffee table. Startled by a sound, I stood at attention surveying the room. The cat poked its head out from behind a chair, its rhinestone-studded color picking up the light.

"Meet Precious."

The cat raised her back, hairs standing on end, and screeched before scooting back down the hall. The suddenness of the outburst put me on edge. "I don't think she like's me." I pulled my sweatshirt down.

"She doesn't take to strangers real easily." Shawna disappeared past a dining room table draped with some kind of lacey tablecloth. That completed the museum-like scene.

I checked out the couch, probably known as a settee. Easing down, I hoped those spindly legs wouldn't collapse under my 185 pound frame. As soon as I sat down, the room closed in on me. I wiped my forehead. Was this claustrophobia? Vertigo settled on me like being at the top of a skyscraper. Was I just feeling the bottle and a half of wine I had consumed? I fought the urge to race out of the room, but held myself taut as Shawna returned and filled two wine goblets with the cabernet. I downed mine in about three gulps. I swallowed letting a bit of tension flow before I grabbed the bottle and refilled the glass.

She just stood there staring at me.

I took another swig before I reached for her hand. As she sat next to me, I finished off the rest of my wine. I leaned over and kissed her neck before reaching for another bottle. I uncorked it and raised my glass. The room and all those pictures began to spin. The Gingerbread clock, chiming, rang in my ears like reverberating echoes.

The last thing I remember was trying to kiss Shawna.

When I opened my eyes, I didn't know where I was. Lying on the floor with my shoes off, I rubbed my eyes. My head ached. I felt woozy. It took a moment to realize that this was Shawna's living room. I stood cautiously, teetering a bit and tried to shake myself awake. Finding my shoes at the side of the couch, I sat back and shoved them on my feet. Heading out to my Jeep, I tried to reconstruct what had happened before I blacked out, pretty sure the evening didn't hold the promise I had hoped it would.

As the sun slowly lightened the morning sky, I wondered if there was any way I could face Shawna again.

Chapter 31

On a Hill Far Away

Shawna called me the next day to see if I was okay. I would be going back to the base in two days. Even though she hinted she'd like to see me, I opted to let it rest. I wasn't sure if my behavior the previous night was brought on by her, if her 'museum' was haunting me, or I was losing it. It just seemed like if things worked out for us, it would have to be when I got past whatever was going on inside my head.

Before I reported back to the base, I wanted to say my farewells. I went by Don and Kelly's house. After some tearful remembrances we hugged. "Let us know when you're back, okay?"

"It'll be sometime in February when I muster out." I waved on my way out to the car. "See You."

Next, I just wanted to talk to Josh, which meant a visit to the Pacific Sunset Cemetery. Unlike the dreary rainy day of the funeral, sun filtered through the old growth spruce as the Jeep rose to the open area. The graves spread around the gentle sloping grade with sunshine spilling across the field.

My heart fluttered when I saw Josh's Mustang parked as I neared the back of cemetery where he was buried. It took a moment to remember it was Jules' too.

There she sat, kneeling by his gravestone. I waited for a moment not wanting to intrude. She turned and motioned me to join her. Snuzz saw her too, tilted his head whining as if to say, "Let's go." When I opened the door, he waited for the signal then sat on the grass until I got out.

With Snuzz at my heels, I trekked across the unmown field of grass and weeds that blanketed the rise obscuring many of the flat grave markers and giving the impression of mournfulness. Snuzz lay down at Jules' side then rested his head on his paws.

As I sat on the other side of her, she reached out and ruffled the dog's fur. Jules drew up her knees, one arm wrapped around them, the other searching for a clover. She plucked one and gently held up. "Look I found a four-leaf clover." She held it up. "Don't you wish there was magic? That my wish would come true?"

I picked a clover, though mine only had three leaves. "I know what you'd wish and I suppose that would also be my wish, however what I'd realistically ask for is that there are some positives that will come from this tragedy."

"At first, I just wanted to die, to be with him. I screamed at God, 'Why? Why don't you take me too?' And do you know what flashed in front of my eyes?"

I shook my head.

"I closed my eyes. A little boy stood holding Josh by the hand. They waved at me and then disappeared as quickly as they appeared." She laid her elbows on her knees leaning her forehead on top letting her dark hair fall around her in a cocoon. "Do you think he will ever come back in a vision to us again?"

"It was amazing how some of the sorrow floated away with the vision. So yeah, I hope so."

"There are reasons…" she sucked in a breath, "…for everything… I just don't see them right now." Her shoulders shook. "And I have a child to think about."

Nothing I could say that would wipe away the tears. I wrapped my arm around her. So we sat for a long while until she composed herself. Then we walked back toward our cars hand in hand. Snuzz walked along beside us, his tail tucked down mirroring the sadness in our hearts.

"I'm taking off tomorrow," I scuffed my feet against the gravel and stared at the ground, trying very hard not to lose it.

"I know. I'll write." She kissed me on the cheek.

I hugged my arms around her not wanting to let go. "That's a promise I'll hold you to."

After she climbed into her Mustang, still pinching the four-leaf clover in her thumb and forefinger, I watched her drive slowly around the bend soon disappearing behind the trees.

I trudged back down the grade sinking next to Josh's gravestone. My dog laid his head on my outstretched legs then snuzzed under my hand. I leaned down to hold him close. He smiled up at me as I scratched his ears. One might think that he just wanted attention, though I think that he has his own way of trying to assuage the sadness as he understands how people are feeling. He knows when they need a gentle touch.

I ran my fingers across the words incised in the polished gray granite stone,

"Joshua James Cole
1985-2010
Beloved Husband, Father,
Son, Friend,
Star and Hero"

I smirked, thinking how Josh had said once, when he became a big businessman, he would be known as JJ Cole. I picked some grass from the edge of the stone and tossed it aside.

"Say, Old Buddy JJ, I just wanted to let you be the first to know. I will not re-up. I am trying to figure out what to do with myself. The one thing I know for sure is that I will be around to help Jules."

I plucked another clover, twirled it around before I noticed that it was also four leafed. How bizarre. One very seldom finds a four-leaf clover, yet we just found two of them in a six-foot square area. I contemplated the rarity of this find and hoped it was portended some thing good. I laid it on Josh's gravestone. "I know I'll never be the father you could have been, but I promise to always be there to remind him that he is the son of the best man I ever knew." I smiled. "I've started to write down stories of our growing up, stories of our missions, so he'll know the real you, the boy, the soldier, the man." I rested my arms on my knees. "Okay, Okay maybe it will be a girl…"

I stood for one last salute before I returned to the car, Snuzz kept close to my side, head down, tail tucked between his legs, simulating my somber mood.

"Okay, Snuzz. What's next for us?

Chapter 32

Leaving Again

The rest of my two days I spent in my room with my new best friend, Jack Daniels. I locked myself in knowing Snuzz camped outside in the hall next to my door. I didn't feel like I deserved to be comforted. I lived, totally unscathed by the brutality of war while my friends were injured or killed, me with nothing but a few scratches and bruises. Why was I still alive? Josh had everything to live for He's gone because of me. Why did I deserve to have Snuzz? Why didn't I give him to a buddy in our platoon that had lost his arm to IED just a few days before Snuzz left?

I started drinking in the morning, passed out in the afternoon woke for another beer or two then lay awake until the middle of the night. Closing my eyes brought on exploding nightmares that jarred me to my soul, I sometimes screamed and other times a cold sweat drenched me in chills. The only time I came out of my room I went for more beer or when the Jack ran out. My mother knocked a few times asking if I was okay or if I was hungry. I ignored her, resented her for knowing that I was succumbing to this weakness. I threw a can at the door.

The next morning I had to leave. I woke up to the smell of Mom's 'Farmer John' breakfast, as she called it, the scent of sizzling bacon wafting down the hall. For the first time in the last couple of days, I felt like eating. It'd be stupid to pass up my last opportunity to eat Mom's home cooking. I scarfed up those pancakes, not forgetting to reward Snuzz with a few tasty tidbits. I was beginning to face the fact that I wouldn't be seeing him for a while, knowing that not having him with me would leave a big hole in my existence. I worried that Jules would have a hard time alone. I hoped her being at school with the children would help her through.

Back in my room I stuffed things in my duffle bag. Snuzz lay glum in the middle of my bed, head on his paws, with his humanoid eyes following my every movement. Once in a while he'd raise one of those crazy ears.

When everything was tucked in and zipped shut I spent a moment on the bed with my arms wrapped around Snuzz. I brushed his fur and realized that this simple act had soothed my shattered nerves of the last couple of days.

"Mom, can we take Snuzz to the airport with us?" I said as I came back to the kitchen with the duffle bag over my shoulder.

"Sure," she said loading the last of the dishes into the dishwasher. "I'll meet you at the car in a minute."

Snuzz followed me out to the garage where I stowed my stuff in the trunk of Mom's Chevy. I led Snuzz out to the back yard, his tail on super speed anticipating the tennis ball I held over him. I threw a quick short one. Snuzz scrambled, managed to leap high and pluck it out of the air. He lit out racing back to me where he dropped the ball into my waiting hand. "Good boy!" I threw the saliva-infested ball a few more times before Mom came out jangling her keys.

"I can drive, Mom."

"Wouldn't you rather spend the time with the dog?"

"Well, maybe so." I opened the back door and signaled Snuzz to hop in. "Mind if I sit in the back with Snuzz?"

"Not at all. I don't mind being replaced in your affections by such a super dog."

Snuzz curled up with his head in my lap. I'm sure he knew this was good-by again. After a nearly silent ride, we approached the Eugene airport.

"Hey, Mom, just drop me off in front after we let Snuzz

stretch his legs." It would be easier to say a quick good-bye than linger. If I brought Snuzz along, we couldn't leave him in the car at the airport very long therefore the goodbyes would be at a minimum. I let Snuzz out to do his business. I scratched his back, the favorite spot right down his backside by his tail, jostled his ears and snuggled his head before giving Mom a hug.

"I'm worried about you, Zack. Are you going to be okay?"

"Not to worry. I'm fine. Just had a sinking spell. If I can't handle it, I'll see somebody – promise." I kissed her cheek and skipped off with a quick salute.

And I truly did believe I was fine.

Chapter 33

Back at Camp Lejeune

Somehow going back to a military routine of keeping fit kept my mind busy for the first couple of weeks or so, but as soon as I started the path to mustering out something changed.

The night brought slashing rain with booms of thunder that prepped my imagination. I fell asleep well enough, but out of nowhere, bombs lit the sky. At first it seemed beautiful. I had the feeling I was at a fireworks show. However, the scene changed instantly. Buildings crumbled all around me. With bullets flying, pinging as they whizzing past my ears, I turned. I ran this way and that way trying to avoid the hailstorm of gunfire closing in on me. Safety. I hurled myself down a blind alley. I ran until I couldn't breathe when I collapsed against the wall. Silence broke like in an eerie movie when you know the victim is still in serious trouble. You know something is out there. Something deadly ominous waits. My every sense heightened. The only sounds I could hear were my heart pounding and my gasps for air. Suddenly the doorways were filled with AK-47's aiming at me, the snarling dark faces of the Taliban yelling, "Allah!" Fire streaked from the barrels. Snuzz lay at my feet in a sea of blood. I screamed at the Taliban attackers. Then came the explosion. As in a slow motion replay, I could see the bullets spinning directly at me. Silent screams contorted my face. I awoke, trembling. I had soiled my sheets. Shame overwhelmed me.

After several fitful nights of reliving some of the worst

scenes of my experiences in Afghanistan, enmeshed with attacks, bombings, snipers lining me in their sights or worse – the bloody fatal attacks of my fellow marines, I knew I needed to seek help. Was I admitting that I had PTSD? No. I had talked with some other guys. If this continued beyond my service, in order to use my Veteran's benefits, I would need to establish a connection to my war experience and establish a written record of the manifestations. A few sleeping pills might just do the trick. I knew that others had sought help here at the base. Their complaints were often dismissed, and they were again deployed. At least I wouldn't have to worry about that.

Nevertheless, I answered the question, "Do you suffer from emotional disturbances that you attribute to your military service?" with a, "yes," I was given a stack of paperwork. I filled this all in before I was assigned an appointment to see the base psychiatrist.

A shrink, who would ever have thought I would go to one voluntarily?

I walked across the quad glancing over my shoulder, furtively watching for anyone I might know. I pulled my cover down over my forehead. I smiled thinking that was a weird name for a military hat, like a manhole cover holding the darkness in.

Pausing a moment before I entered, I turned the handle and walked in. The typical spare, drab military office did nothing to assuage my tension. I paced the floor for a while before settling in to a wooden seat. I waited, spinning my cover in my hands until I was about to leave. At that moment, I was called in. I felt tense like I had stuck my finger into a light socket.

I stood at attention. The doc wore a kindly sense of concern on his lined face. "At ease." He gestured to the chair opposite him. "Sit down, Langston." Behind his desk the sun streamed in through the window casting a glow through his gray crew cut.

I looked around expecting to see a couch. There wasn't one.

A sense of vertigo overtook me as I sank into the chair where the Doctor directed me.

"Relax. We're just going talk. Tell me, Zack, what brings you to see me?"

I glanced down, through the window, anywhere but into his eyes. I explained the dreams, the depression, the guilt and the vertigo that often took me by surprise.

It was the first I had admitted my frailties to anyone, my weaknesses and worse – my fear. By the time I had finished describing my symptoms, I felt incredibly drained and exhausted.

"Mind if I ask you a few questions?"

"No, Sir." This time our eyes connected.

Had I experienced these episodes during my waking daylight hours? No. Had I become violent? No, not unless you count knocking a few things off my dresser that one time. Attacked anyone? No. Was I paranoid? No. Did I go for periods of time without any of these dreams? Yes. Have I been drinking? Yes. Can you get along without drinking? Yes. Are you an alcoholic? No. Can you carry out your duties? Yes. So the questions went.

Many of his questions got me analyzing my own situation and rationalizing.

He leaned back in his chair, elbows on the arms of his chair, and placed his hands in front of him, fingertips touching like a spider on a mirror. "What you have faced in Afghanistan inflicted an horrendous assault on your psyche. The reactions you describe are quite normal for a number of returning soldiers. These symptoms will ease off in time. Though I can see why you were concerned. These thoughts are disturbing."

He scrutinized my chart. "You're a very fit Marine with a stellar record. You should be very proud."

"Just a mild sedative you can take if you are having a rough night. This is an antidepressant. These will help." He handed me two plastic pill bottles.

Strangely I felt better, much better. The tension had eased. Maybe all I needed was just to talk it over with someone, someone I didn't know. That was it.

Everything was fine. Just fine.

I whistled as I strode out of the office.

Chapter 34

Demons

Barely a week passed before the dreams started again. At first I resisted taking the pills the doctor gave me. Then sometimes I forgot how many I took.

I didn't leave the base after I first got back. I had a tough time going into town since my return. The recollection of the night when the accident took Josh haunted me, but with a weekend pass and nothing to do, I caught a ride in town with some of the guys.

We hit the V Bar just after the sun went down. The first beer went down easy. After that, I knocked them back so fast that I barely differentiated between the first bar and several others we hit before heading back to the base. The next thing I remember was waking up the next morning the four of us sacked out in the car. At least I didn't dream.

Two subsequent weekends passed the same way except I had moved on to Jack Daniels as my best friend. It didn't occur to me that the other guys were fighting their own demons, that maybe we could talk about it.

Now I faced the biggest demon of all, going back to Florence. Shawna wrote me a couple of times. Without an answer, her letters dropped off.

Jules' sister Connie and her niece came. They now lived with her. I felt better Jules wasn't alone even though her sister also needed help. Being needed is sometimes a comfort. Connie's husband had left her and their little girl, emptied their bank account, drove away in their car, which left them with nothing but bills. They had no idea where he was. Connie didn't even have a job. The plan was that if she didn't find a job, Jules would pay her to baby sit when the baby was born.

I eagerly anticipated mail from Jules and managed to answer a few of hers. Pinned up side-view pictures of her lined my locker like a time-lapse progress of her pregnancy. Watching her stomach grow was the highlight of my weeks. I was surprised that only a few weeks made a noticeable difference in her girth. Jules' niece apparently was lifting both their spirits. I pasted a picture of the laughing cherub next to the ones of Jules.

As much as I wanted to go home, the thought of actually living a normal life, hunting for a job, having my mother witness my weakness, and especially being the rock that Jules might need totally unnerved me. I dismissed the idea that I had a problem, that I was dependent on the pills or booze, despite the fact that the dreams intensified, even with the pills.

The uncertainty that I could handle all of it played havoc with my mind.

I booked a last session with the psychiatrist. He refilled my prescriptions then sent me off with a recommendation to visit the VA facility in Roseburg.

I was headed for Oregon but where was my life headed? The only thing I knew was that I would have to figure it out in the next few days.

Chapter 35

Thinking It Through

I wanted to take my promise to Josh seriously. I needed to be around, now more than ever, with a baby due in August. Juliana would need all the help she could get. However, I couldn't be there for her if I didn't get my life squared away.

I felt a sadness settle in. Being a Marine was so much a part of me. Would I no longer feel as alive as I had felt, awaking every morning knowing that I had purpose and order in my life?

It seemed I couldn't get time alone with my thoughts until I got on the plane home to Oregon. I gave myself a mental pat on the back for being very frugal by saving up a pretty good bank account in the last four years. I made myself a list of things to do like getting a job and finding an apartment while I thought about what I wanted to do with my life besides figure out what to do between slugs of Jack. I had heard that jobs might be tough to get, unemployment soared high as employers became leery of soldiers returning with their heads all messed up. I smirked at the thought of me fitting the profile.

I liked to write. In high school I took Journalism because my girlfriend talked me into it. However, the class became one of my favorites. In my college freshman year I wrote for the newspaper at the U of O. Now I constantly wrote stories about Josh to save for his child. Maybe the Siuslaw News would give me a chance. A vision of a 1940's reporter with a press sign stuck in his fedora brought a smile. This wasn't what I planned for a career, but I needed to support myself so I could move out of Mom's place.

Drowsiness set it. Almost as soon as I shut my eyes, a dust

storm headed my way. Images of Taliban sneaking behind with rifles poking through the brown haze invaded my sleep. I was backing away when I recoiled and stifled a scream. The stewardess had awakened me by she touching my shoulder as she reached for my empty glass. I woke with a jerk, knocking her hand away.

"Sorry I startled you." She stepped back to pick up the empty glass where I had knocked it out of her hand. "We're almost there." She wandered down the aisle collecting plastic glasses, snack debris and putting them into a white plastic trash bag.

That was the longest sleep I had in a while, like a baby who sleeps during a ride in a vehicle. Maybe I should just buy a plane, hire a pilot, and fly around all the time.

Mom met the plane. After a big hug she said, "I'll pull the car around front. Snuzz came too so I don't want to leave him too long in the car."

She hurried off. I waved as I headed to the luggage carousel.

Waiting for my duffle bag and backpack to come down the chute onto to the conveyer, I thought about Jules. I had seen the pictures of her, but the last time I saw her she was still skinny. I regretted not telling her about me coming home. I know she would've come. It proved to be an empty homecoming without her here. I visualized her waiting for me with arms outstretched as I exited the plane like so many other passengers had waiting for them. It was my fault since I specifically told Mom not to tell anyone. Since Josh was gone, she and Snuzz were my best friends.

A girl I had seen on the plane stood next to me watching the carousel circle around with lumps of cases and boxes. She reached for her huge bag, but it got away from her before she could grab it. I dashed ahead and plucked it off. "Here you go." I sat it down in front of her.

"Thanks," she said smiling up at me, creating big deep dimples in her freckled cheeks. She grunted while she barely lifted the suitcase with both hands.

"Let me."

“Thanks,” she said pushing some red curls out of her face.

I carried it out to the sidewalk for her. “Do you need a ride?”

“No, my boyfriend’s coming. Thanks anyway.”

“Sure.” I gave her a little salute, suddenly realizing I had gotten into that habit but I was not in the corps anymore. That was my first realization that even though, ‘once a Marine always a Marine’, I was actually a civilian. I wasn’t sure I knew how to leave my organized life behind.

I guess I was glad that the ‘Annie’ look-alike didn’t expect any more small talk or actually want a ride, as I seemed to have lost my ability to communicate with more than a few words.

By the time I had retrieved my luggage and had come back out front, the girl was gone. I wondered if her boyfriend had let her put that heavy suitcase in the trunk by herself.

Mom pulled the Chevy up to the curb. Snuzz circled in the back seat pawing the window. I could hear his whine clear though the closed car window.

“You better get in back with him,” Mom said as I stowed my gear in the trunk and slammed the trunk shut.

I could barely scoot Snuzz over to get in, hand signals or no. Guess he was too excited.

“Quit your whining.” He leaped at my face just to make sure he licked just about every whisker. “Okay, okay.” Wrapping my arms around him, I buried my face in his fur.

At home, I headed for the refrigerator, no beer.

I got the hint, not sure if I appreciated that or not. Now I had to make a conscious effort… A cold February chill gave me a quick shiver. I could do it.

Chapter 36
Adjusting

On the quiet ride home, I couldn't get Jules out of my mind. So after taking Snuzz for a long walk on the beach, I hopped in my Jeep and headed to her house, knowing she'd be home from school by the time I got there.

Jules' sister, Connie, greeted me at the door. I hadn't taken much notice of her at the funeral. A few years younger than Jules, I remembered her as the little sister who always tagged along. She pestered us when we had our secret club meetings in the tree house, and always wanted to go to the show with us. She led down the aisle as a junior bridesmaid at the wedding. When she got pregnant, she left home. Now she had grown into a woman, nearly as beautiful as Jules. She swished a dark braid over her shoulder appearing sadder than I had ever seen her.

"Hi, Zack." She gave me a quick hug.

A tot with brown curly hair held Connie's hand, looking up at me, "Who are you?"

I did a double take at how well the child spoke considering how small she was. She stuck her palm up at me so I gave her a high-five. "I'm Zack. And who are you?"

"My name is Katy and I don't like my other name." She struggled to hold up four fingers. "I'm four. How old are you?"

"Okay Katherine. Yeah, she's four going on 14. Come in." Connie gestured. Jules just got home from work. She's changing. She'll be right out."

"Who is it?" Jules hollered in."

"You'll see. Hurry up."

"I'm just washing my face. Be there in a minute."

"Why don't you sit down?"

I wandered over to the couch, picked up the redheaded doll, scooted it aside, and sat.

"That's Poopsie Lu. She's mine. Wanna play?"

Before I could answer, Katy popped up on the couch and plunked herself on my lap. She pretended that Poopsie Lu whispered in her ear. "Poopsie Lu wants to know if you want some tea?" She leaned almost out of my lap, reached over to the coffee table for a tiny cup and handed it to me. She took the other one.

I slurped loudly. "That's just delicious."

Jules came in twisting her long dark hair into ponytail. "Hey! Zack!"

She took my breath away, standing there all plump and freshly scrubbed. I stood up so quickly I grabbed for Katy. "Wouldn't want do to drop you on the floor." I lifter her up under her arms, stood and swung her around before setting her in front of her mom.

"Let's do that again." Katy reached both arms up to me.

"Maybe later, Katy."

"Let's go, Honey. There's a game I want to show you in our room." Connie took Katy's hand. They disappeared down the hallway.

"Jules!" I practically tripped on the coffee table while circling it to throw my arms around her. "Let me look at you." I held her away from me. Staring at her small round belly. "Could I?" I reached out.

"Sure."

I softly rubbed.

"There's no Genie in there, you know." As she sat on the couch, she patted. "Come. Sit. Let me show you the pictures, my ultra sounds." She opened a small photo album. "This is at 3 months." She pointed at the black and white image. "This one is just last week. Can you tell?"

"Tell what?"

"It's a boy. See right there?"

"A boy!" I stared wide-eyed. "It's boy! Yes!" I thrust my hand in the air.

Chapter 37

Food for Thought

On the way home, I stopped by the Siuslaw Newspaper office and slipped into the parking place right in front. Standing in front of the reception area, I rested my forearms on the counter overlooking the front desk.

A round pleasant girl glanced up from her computer to ask, "May I help you?"

"I'm looking for work. I'd like an application, please."

"Just a moment." She ambled to the back of the office. Before she returned, she spoke with someone there. "Here ya go." She handed me the application. "Not sure we need anyone right now. Go ahead and fill one out anyway."

"Thanks, I'll bring it back tomorrow. Something may come up."

"Sure."

I stopped for a six-pack and a bottle of Jack. I rationalized that I hadn't experienced any vertigo or claustrophobia for a while. A little celebration couldn't hurt, a boy is on its way, plus I took a step toward being a civilian again.

When I opened the back door at home, Mom had a pot roast in the oven with the smell wafting into the mudroom, just waiting to lure me in. I put the beer in the fridge and the Jack in the cupboard.

"Are you sure that's a good idea?"

I examined the bottle as I closed the door. "Yeah…well. Hey! I have some news!"

"What news?"

I popped the top of a Coors. "I stopped by Jules' place."

"She's okay?"

"Yeah, sure. She showed me the ultrasound and...it's a boy!"

"That's wonderful!" Mom said as she took the roast out of the oven, reached over to set it to the side on the trivet.

I grabbed a hot pad, lifted the lid sending the rich scent of the roast rising up with the steam. I peeked into the roast pan with browned potatoes smiling up at me. I sucked in another whiff. "Wow! That smells so good."

"Would you set the table while I dish up?"

I reached for the plates and set the silverware out. Mom spooned out the potatoes that she had cooked in with the roast. I practically drooled as she got the salads from the fridge. I hadn't been that hungry since the last homecoming.

"I stopped at the newspaper. Got an application. I've always enjoyed writing. I am hoping they could use a cub reporter."

"Wow. You're not even taking a vacation."

"They haven't hired me yet. Besides, I had a vacation the last time I came home, which, in case you have forgotten, was only a couple of months ago."

"There's lot's of stuff going on in this town to write about." Mom sat opposite me at the kitchen table.

"I bet. The city council meetings and the maybe the inside skinny on the VFW happenings." I shoveled in a mouthful of potatoes. "This is great, Mom."

"Well, we actually had a bank robbery in Mapleton." Mom wiped the napkin across her face. "And we do have concerts and plays. The Casino is here now. They really get name entertainment."

"I thought I'd dust off a few of the sports stories I wrote for the college paper maybe tweak 'em a bit. I also have some short stories, stories about Josh that I have been writing for his son." I twirled my fork in the air. "His son! I can hardly wait to have a game of catch with him." I grabbed another slab of roast beef and scooped some more potatoes on my plate. "Also I wrote a couple of articles for the Camp Leatherneck paper that they might actually consider as journalism."

"I've always thought you'd be good at writing, what with some of those things you wrote in high school. Remember sometimes, when I was busy I'd have you write your own excuse for being absent."

"Sometimes I was truly sick. I didn't always stick my thermometer on the light bulb." I scraped up the last of the potatoes then forked another helping of roast on my plate.

"I remember one night you wanted me to write you a note as I chatted on the phone. I told you to go write one and I would sign it. So you disappeared into your room." Mom took her last bite of salad and munched. "You returned with the note - three pages long about how you had started riding to school along Rhododendron Drive. The wind swept you off your bicycle and threw you into the channel of the Siuslaw River, how you were dashed against the rocks then finally managed to latch onto a log that floated you to out to sea - in shark infested waters."

"Oh, I remember. That's the one where I said I got picked up by a Chinese cargo ship and forced into hard labor?"

"When you escaped, you stole a Chinese junk and sailed home just in time for school."

"I think you missed a page or two in your synopsis, Mom. I guess I'll gather some stories up. They'll be so impressed they'll have to hire me." I would have licked my plate if I hadn't scraped it so clean. "Fantastic dinner, Mom. Thanks."

She smiled as she watched me rinse the dishes and put them in the dishwasher. "Well, the Marines taught you something! Anyway, I saved that note in case you want to take it in with your application."

"That oughta really do it, Mom."

I took a couple of beers and headed for my room to find the stories and sort through them.

"If you want to take that application by tomorrow, maybe you should go easy..."

"Yeah, yeah, yeah."

Chapter 38

Endings are Beginnings

In my room, the dust swirled when I dragged my old notebooks off the bookshelf. I found one feature story I had written about a 10th grader who suffered a bout with cancer and came successfully through the chemo treatments. I considered it one of my better stories. I searched my laptop for a story I had written just before leaving Afghanistan, the last mission where my team destroyed the munitions plant. If I revamped these pieces to fit the criteria for a news story, just maybe the paper might consider me.

I sat down at the computer, analyzing before I pounded out variations of the stories until I thought they were a fair representation of my writing skills.

When I finished, Snuzz lifted his snout, stretched checking me out like, "Okay, are you done yet?"

"Yeah, Old Pal." I dove at him. We roughhoused on the floor rolling around until he was lolling on his back with his tongue hanging out getting his last rub down.

I had been so busy, I had forgotten about the beers that sat unopened on the end of my desk.

"It's late, Snuzz," I said as I stripped down to my shorts. Standing at the side of the bed, I plunked my hands on my hips. "Hey! Move over you big hog." I pushed Snuzz aside and hopped in. Spreading out, I felt pretty proud of myself for getting back into the swing of things. Snuzz gave me his good night slurpy kiss and settled next to me. The world was right again.

Waking the next morning, after a great night's sleep, I found an old leather portfolio in the hall closet. I wasn't sure where it came from or what it was used for, but it had the appearance of something professional. Not knowing, these days, if applying for a job was done online or with a CD, I burned a CD with my stories on it. I still figured an in-person-delivery carried more weight that anything impersonal online. Maybe I'd be lucky enough to catch the editor so I could wow her with my enthusiasm, which I would work on in the next hour during my shower, shave and breakfast.

"Mom, I can't be eating one of these 'Farmer John' breakfasts every morning, at least until I join a gym!" I sat down to waffles with ham and eggs. Snuzz enjoyed his portion too, but I knew not to keep this up with him either.

Cruising along in my Jeep, I appreciated driving again, though I found I really had to watch myself as the speedometer kept inching up. I hoped the sun filled sky was a good omen.

I found a parking space opposite the office, hesitated a moment then hustled across the street to the Siuslaw News office.

I lucked out. Ms. Bauer and I met each other in the entrance of the office. "Do you have a moment, Ms. Bauer?

She studied me. "Sure, a minute is about all, but... sure, come on in." She was all business with her short-cropped grey hair and sturdy frame as she edged behind her desk. "Sit down."

With my hands shaking, I sat down wondering if I could really do this.

"What can I do for you?" She leafed through some papers on her in front of her.

"Well... I'm Zachary Langston." I set my portfolio on her desk, subtracted the stories with the application. "Now that my tour of duty with the Marines is over, I need a job. And I'm pretty good at writing." I handed the papers to her.

She looked me directly in the eye. "Yesterday I would have said, 'We don't need anyone now,' but one of our reporters got a job with a bigger paper near Portland. She's leaving in two weeks."

"Here's a CD, if you'd prefer." I handed it across to her.

"I've had a little experience writing for the base newspaper. One of the stories is in there."

"Let me check this over and we'll see what I can do."

"I'd appreciate it."

"Thanks. And if you'll excuse me." She stood then walked around the desk. "I enjoyed meeting you, Zachary. I'll get back with you soon."

"Thank you for your time, Ms. Bauer."

I walked out whistling thinking this had been easier than I could've hoped for.

Chapter 39

A Road Trip

The next couple of days, my positive expectations had me strategizing. Keeping in shape helped my mental attitude. I went for runs on the beach, spent a night or two at the Beachcomber perhaps drinking more than I should, but I could control it.

Maybe Monday I would hear from the paper.

I hated to leave Snuzz for a whole day. We had been inseparable with five-mile runs everyday. But I promised an outing Saturday morning. Jules and Katy wanted to go for a trip to the Zoo, the Game Park Safari in Bandon. Connie had a couple of appointments for employment at some of the local restaurants and bars, so we were Katy's sitters for the day.

Standing with my arms outstretched, I took in the warm rays of the sun noting that there wasn't much wind. Thinking Katy would get a kick out of having the top down, I lowered the top on the Jeep. The heater going with the windows rolled up made it pretty confortable. We could always put it up as we got going fast out of town.

I drove up in front of Jules' place about 10:00AM, just as Jules came out holding the car seat in one hand and swinging hands with Katy.

Her curly pigtails bounced as Katy skipped along. "This looks like a Matchbox car," Katy patted the fender.

"Wait a minute, Katy, until Uncle Zack gets the seat installed." Jules passed me the car seat.

"Okay." Katy sat on the curb whispering secrets to Poopsie Lu who was taking her first trip to a zoo.

"So you think I know how to put one of these things in properly."

"Let me show you..." Jules took the seat securing it in back.

"Thanks." I caught on pretty quickly. We had it installed in no time.

"I've never been in a car with no lid on it before." Katy hopped in back and I buckled her in.

"Thought you'd like it. Let me know if you get cold. We can put the top up."

Taking it slowly through town, Katy giggled at the wind in her face, but as we passed the turn off to West Lake, we decided to put up the top.

"Do we have to?" Katy begged.

"I'm so cold." I gave an exaggerated shiver. "Pleeeeze?"

"O...kaaay. Poopsie Lu is cold, too."

Jules grinned at me. "You remember when we were kids and your mom took us up to the Tillamook Factory?"

"Yeah. What was the name of that game we played, 'I Spy With My Little Eye'. I wonder if Katy would like to play that game?"

"Want to play a game, Poopsie Lu?" Katy made the doll's voice high-pitched. "Yes!"

"I go first." I blurted out. "First I will think of something in the car. I will describe it without telling you what it is. You can ask questions, like what color is it? Is it big or small? First one who guesses what it is gets the next turn. Ready."

"Ready," came the high-pitched voice. "Poopsie Lu is ready," Katy said.

"I spy with my little eye, something that has pigtails." Now that sounded pretty easy to guess except there were three girls in the car that had pigtails.

Jules surreptitiously caught my eye and pointed to herself.

I shook my head.

"Is it me?" Jules asked.

"No."

Katy felt her own pigtails. "What color is it?"

It ran through my mind how sharp Katy as she asked that question. "Red."

"Poopsie Lu." Her giggle had us all laughing.

"You're so smart! Okay it's your turn. Remember not to tell us what it is."

Without being reminded what to say, she said, "I spy with my little eye something black."

"The steering wheel?" I said.

"No."

"What shape is it?" Jules asked.

"Round."

I made a couple of wrong guesses.

"The gear shift?" Jules pointed to the knob.

"Uh...Yes!"

We played the game until we came to Coos Bay where we stopped at MacDonald's for a burger, coke and fries. Jules and I chatted while we watched Katy play on the kid's play equipment.

"We better go before Katy gets too tired for the zoo."

Out on the road Katy asked the universal kid's question. "When are gonna be there?" Then her eyes got heavy and she napped all the way past Bandon until we arrived at the Game Park.

After persuading Katy through the gift shop, she rushed in and skipped right after one of the peacocks. I intercepted her and whisked her up on my shoulders. "You scare the animals when you chase them."

Just then one of the peacocks fanned his tail feathers. "Oh look!" She giggled. Then the donkey came close and brayed, "Hee Haw!" She imitated him. "Hee Haw."

One of the docents asked if Katy would like to come into the petting zoo, where they had a baby wolf. The docent held the baby letting Katy feed the wolf pup with a bottle. I took out my iPhone and snapped the cutest picture of Katy kissing the baby wolf on its head.

The way she ran from animal cage to animal cage, clapping, talking to the creatures and jumping up and down when they moved, we surmised she had never been to a zoo before.

"Let's go home." Jules and I grabbed her hands so we could give her a swing between us.

"Do we have to go?"

"Don't you think Poopsie Lu is lonesome in the car?" I said. "Besides, I think there's something waiting for you in the gift shop."

I bought Katy a little stuffed wolf, which she introduced to Poopsie Lu as Wolf Boy. During our ride home she carried on a conversation between the two of her toys until she slumped to the side and fell asleep.

"She's a great kid. I never thought I liked kids, much." I raised my eyebrows.

"Well, maybe you just fooled yourself, because you're great with her."

On the way home, Jules and I talked about her pregnancy. "My sister and I are going to do the Lamaze exercise class that I ordered on line. The set of DVD's is due to come soon."

"What a fun day," I said as I let them out at Jules' place.

"You stay with us." Katy pulled at my hand.

"I can't today, but I'll come back."

"Promise?"

"Cross my heart." I gestured.

When she started to cry, Jules picked her up and carried her into the house. "She's a tired girl."

As I hopped back into the Jeep, I realized it had been a full day without depression or anxiety, not even one time.

Chapter 40

Not So Easy

On Monday, I got a call from the Siuslaw Newspaper to meet with Ms. Bauer in the afternoon.

I hadn't been that excited for a long time. I showered in a hurry. Not sure what to wear, I took a clue from how casual everyone was there in the office. I pulled on a pair of Dockers and buttoned up my blue Polo shirt.

On my way there, I pictured me sitting through exciting high school games, writing riveting sports news or maybe reviewing some of the performances that were coming up at the Florence Event Center. Anticipation rose high.

I parked a few doors back and walked in whistling. With her door so near the entrance and her office right close to the front counter, Ms. Bauer immediately invited me in. She gestured to the chair. I sat down in front of her desk.

She rested her elbows on the desk. "I reviewed the material you submitted, Zackary."

"Zack, if you don't mind, Ms. Bauer."

"Okay, Zack." She touched my folder of work. "It's not bad."

"Thanks," I said though wishing she had heaped more praise my way.

She leaned back in her chair. "I'm not prepared to offer you a full time position right now."

I gulped but tried not to let my face sag.

"What I'd like to offer you is a chance to submit stories or to accept assignments as a free lance writer. Are you interested?"

"How does that work?"

"We don't take articles on spec like some other publications might. If you have an idea for a story, you need to run it by me first.

"And an assignment?"

"I would give you an assigned story and have an agreement with you, give you a deadline, indicate a word count, establish pay, and so forth. On assigned stories with photos, you would get a by-line. If the story is substandard, there is no pay. If we retain it for future use, you would be paid. We don't pay extra for the photos, but photos are expected."

I ran my hand over my crew cut.

"We need to cover my concerns first, so please don't take offense. Before I assign a story, these are the rules."

She paused eying me directly.

"Material must be completely original. Plagiarism is illegal. That means any published document or the info from Internet sources may not be copied. We have a zero tolerance policy. Photographs must be taken by you or have written permission from the photographer. Digital photos must be of a good enough quality for publication."

"How would I submit my work?"

"Stories are to be submitted electronically – text documents need to be attached as an email and it's a good idea to imbed them as well. Stories must be one hundred percent factual and you need to make sure they are fact checked. There is no staff to proof read or to check your accuracy. We have a reputation to protect. Therefore we have to be very strict. You also need to know that the story may be cut or altered to fit the needs of the paper."

"I see," I scooched back in my seat.

"You might want to check some back issues of some of our publications like Senior Pride, The Wave, Progress, for ideas for stories you might want to do on your own. Meanwhile I would like to assign a story, which would require you to attend the regular meeting of the Port of Siuslaw with the city manager. Would you be interested?"

I stammered my interest and she laid out the particulars while I took notes. She retrieved some copies of the old issues she had mentioned and handed them to me on the way out.

Okay, so I wouldn't be the star reporter, and I couldn't support myself with this yet, yet it offered a chance to prove myself or at least find out two things. Was I interested in this type of work and was I good at it?

I picked up a couple of six packs and some Jack Daniels then I stopped off at Freddies where I found a mini tape recorder in the electronics department.

Chapter 41

Let's Celebrate

On my way home, I phoned Jules to let her know I'd be coming by. "Hey, wanna grab a couple of beers and celebrate?" "Sure. A beer sounds good for you, but coke's the strongest I drink for me and baby Cole. "Celebrate what?"

"Yeah. Well, I didn't get a full time job at the paper like I expected, but I did get an assignment."

"Congratulations. What's your assignment?"

"I'm going to impress the heck out of Ms. Bauer with a rousing story about the regular Meeting at the Siuslaw Port, all in 400 words or less."

I remember you could always write. Your letters were a kick, but I don't expect they want that journalistic style in a news story."

"Thanks for the pep talk. I'll pick you up in a few. Bye."

Jules bounced down the walkway with her ponytail swaying behind her before she hopped in the jeep.

"Whew! What a great day I had!" She opened the door and slid in.

"Yeah?" I pulled away from the curb.

"I got a new boy in my class, a really shy little guy. Jordon was having a tough day or two adjusting. So yesterday, I took him aside trying to find out a little more about him. When I found out he really liked to play kickball, I decided PE that day would be kickball. I made Jordon a captain. Not only was he pretty good at assigning positions, he could really blast the heck out of that ball."

"I forgot how much fun I used to have playing kickball." I patted Jules tummy. "Maybe we can play that someday."

"I think it'll be a while before he'll be as good as Jordon." She smoothed her top over the round of her abdomen. "Anyway, today, I gave the kickball to Jordon at lunch recess. Afterward, all the kids lined up laughing I saw that Jordon stood right in the middle. 'Let's do that every lunch recess.' They all cheered." Jules pushed a strand of hair out of her eyes. "I wish it could be that easy all the time. Some kids just don't fit in. It takes a lot longer to help them."

"Those experiences must give you a lot of satisfaction."

"That's why I teach."

We drove up, lucky to find a place right in front of the Beachcomber. On the way in, Jules wrapped an arm around me and gave a quick squeeze.

Things were right in my world. It was good to be home.

"Two Coors." I signaled the bartender as we walked past and found seats near the pool table. "Oops. One Coors, one cola."

Jules resembled a princess sitting in that wing chair when Debbie set the beer and cola down in front of us. Thoughts of times when we three came here rolled through my mind. The three of us had been such a team.

"To your new assignment." Jules raised her glass and we clinked. I chugged a couple of gulps. Jules caught me eying the pool table.

She sipped her soda. "Did you want to play?"

"Uh..." I slugged down a couple more slurps. "I don't think so."

"I know what you're thinking. We used to come in here with Josh. I've been trying to make myself come to some of the old places. You know..." She wiped some condensation from her glass. "We can't live here and stay away from everything." She reached for my hand and gave it a squeeze.

I finished off my Coors then smirked, " I suppose we could lock ourselves in the house." I raised two fingers for Debbie to bring two more.

Jules turned to Debbie. "Not for me. I'm still working on this one." She focused her green eyes directly into mine. "Help me on this, Zack. Help me, help us make new memories."

"It won't erase the old ones."

"Those memories are what make us who we are and I don't want to erase them, just mesh them with new ones."

"I didn't tell you that...that...that night..." I shook my head. "...his last night, Josh and I were playing pool. He had snookered a guy into a game. He took his twenty in less than ten minutes."

"He always was the best, wasn't he?"

"That happened just minutes before..." My throat closed and I couldn't speak.

We sat there silently staring at the table. When the new beer came I half emptied it and let out a huge sigh. When I noticed her, her eyes were brimming.

"Come on." She took my hand as she rose out of her seat. "Let's play a game. You and I."

I followed her to the table.

She handed me the triangle. "You rack 'em. I'll break."

Jules leaned over the table, swished her ponytail over to the other shoulder, aimed the cue ball and blasted the balls. They flew in all directions with the red striper dropping in the end pocket. She tipped two more in before she missed.

"Not so bad for a girl. Let me show you how the boys do it." I lined up a bank shot with my solid red ball going straight for the pocket then banging back and forth coming to rest on the lip.

"I think I'll just play like a girl." The only good shot she had, she needed to put the cue behind her back to get the right angle.

We laughed when she missed by almost falling over. I caught her in my arms. Still she had managed to knock in a different ball.

Jules was right. By the time we were down to the last two

balls on the table, we were laughing. At least she was when she banked the eight ball in the side pocket and beat me.

"Next game is mine."

"Yeah, right!"

I did win that one. "Do a tie breaker?"

She shook her head. "I have to get home. Hey! Connie is making spaghetti for dinner. That's a lot of food for three. Why don't you come back to the house?"

"Thanks. I told Mom I wouldn't be home. So I guess I'd just be passing up a PB and J if I declined."

"We have to get a bottle of champagne. Connie has some news she wants to celebrate, besides your celebration."

"Lots to pay tribute to tonight."

As we back to her house, we stopped and I bought a bottle of champagne and a bottle of sparkling apple cider.

The fog rolled in, nestling around the trees, not like the harbinger of gloom, but the soft settling of the fun evening ahead.

Chapter 42

New Beginnings

As we drove up to Jules' place, Katy pulled the curtain aside. Her cupid face peered out the front window. In seconds she ran out the front door toward us.

"Uncle Zack!"

I gathered her up and swung her around. Jules and I each took a hand to swing her between us a few times.

"Don't worry he's staying for dinner."

"Goodie. We're havin' pasketti and Wolf boy wants to see you." She squeezed my hand.

We entered the brightly lit kitchen filled with the fragrance of Italian herbs and garlic, the sauce steaming away on the stove.

By the sink, Jules started chopping up some greens for salad. She pushed a strand of hair out of her face with her wrist. "Want to set the table?"

"Sure." I placed the plates around then grabbed a handful of silverware.

"I wanna help." Katy reached her hands up.

"Okay, you put these forks on this side of all the plates." I followed her around depositing the knives and spoons. I handed her some napkins. "I bet you can put theses right on top of the forks."

Jules put the salad on the table. "Would you mind opening the champagne? I guess Connie has some news for us to celebrate too." She crooked her finger. When I came close she whispered, "You know you got the silverware backwards."

"So." I aimed the bottle at Jules who put her hands up in front of her.

"Don't you dare!"

I safely pointed away. Pop. The cork shot out toward the wall.

"What was that? Poopsie Lu doesn't like loud noises."

I smiled thinking that I don't like loud noises any more either. As the champagne cork made a loud noise, it didn't jar me because I expected it. I stood there with the frosty bottle foaming over the edge. "The champagne pops because it's always happy when we let it out of the bottle. So out it pops. Up comes the foam." I set the champagne flutes on the table and filled them with champagne for Connie and I. I grabbed the sparkling cider. "Is it okay for Katy to have hers in a flute?"

"This doesn't topple so easy." Connie handed me a cute little stemmed glass. " This is her special glass. Not too full, now."

"Here you go. To me, the newly employed journalist." We clicked glasses.

We held our plates while Connie dished up the pasta and piled the meatballs and sauce on top.

Settled at the table, Connie put her napkin in her lap. She patted it down. "Well, I have good news and bad. Good news is I have a job starting this weekend, Saturday night. Bad news is that it is at Ona's in Yachats but I don't have a car."

"Well..." Jules scratched her chin. "A car? We can check around for one, but I don't know if we can get one by Saturday. I guess you could drive mine."

"I stopped by that open field by Heceta Beach Road. You know, where they have a few cars for sale?"

"And?" Jules rolled some spaghetti around her fork and took a bite.

Katy picked up a single strand of noodle, sucked it into her mouth already lined with red marinara sauce, and I tried not to laugh during this serious discussion.

"I have 200 dollars in my suitcase I was saving just in case…when I told him that I was Jules' sister, he said he knew Josh. And the man said if I could give him $300, I could make payments to him until it was paid off. " She leaned her chin on her hands. Any suggestions how I could earn a hundred bucks by Saturday?"

"Want to wax my Jeep?"

"Are you serious? Yeah. I'll wax your Jeep."

"And vacuum it out?"

She nodded. "It'll take a lot of work because I haven't done it since I joined the Marines."

"Absolutely I can do it. Hey, I'll even do the seats and polish the dashboard."

"Consider it done!" I lifted my glass. "Prost! To the newly employed!"

We all took a sip or in my case a gulp.

"You can start polishing as soon as you are able."

"Would you really? Oh, thank you, Zack."

"Now all I need to do is find me a full time job!"

It felt good to be able to help someone who really needed it.

At home, I grabbed a couple of beers before I headed to my room. "Night, Mom."

Everything was going so well. I just didn't remember that things could change in an instant.

Chapter 43

A Transaction

. I remember how much I appreciated holding a hundred dollar bill. So in the morning, I drove to the Siuslaw Bank for the $100 I had promised Connie. When I picked her up, Katy came running out in front of Connie who carried the car seat in front of her.

"Let me have that. I am expert at installing these things now." I had the seat in place in no time. "Here you go." I swung Katy into the seat and buckled her up.

"See." She held up the wolf puppet we got at Bandon Game Park. "Wolf Boy wants the top down."

"Sorry," I reached in and pinched her nose. "It's too foggy. Wolf Boy might catch a cold."

"Ooo-Kay." Her lower lip protruded about an inch.

When Connie got in, I handed her the hundred-dollar bill. "Here's your Benjamin."

"Wow," I don't think I have ever seen a hundred dollar bill let alone hold one. I almost hate to spend it so fast." She studied the front. "So Benjamin Franklin is on the hundred."

"I had thought about writing up a contract for you polishing my car however, can I trust you to drop back at my place and work off your debt?"

She laughed. "I'll be there. Can we come over right after the big deal?" She flipped her braid out from her jacket where it was trapped under the collar. "Do you know anything about cars?"

"I haven't worked on one for a long time. I can walk around the car, examine it like an expert so I so the guy won't think he can get away with anything."

The blue Ford Escort sat in front of the lot. Skirting the edge of which, the rope with multicolored plastic triangles flapped in the breeze. We stepped up to peruse the vehicle.

"What do you think?"

"Well, it's shiny and the color matches your eyes." I said circling the car. I made my way around to open the hood. "It doesn't look like it's ever been in an accident."

"The man is coming." She whispered. "If you took it for a test drive you could listen, see if sounds and feels okay. "I'd really appreciate it you would go in with me when I sign the papers to make sure everything goes right."

I nodded as the bow-legged man headed toward us. He pushed his hands through a gray mop of hair.

"Hi Connie," He turned to me. I'm Axel Richards." He stuck out his hand.

"Zack Langston." We shook. "I understand you knew my friend Josh."

"He used to buy parts from me for that old Mustang of his. Good kid. Sorry about what happened."

I checked out the ground and kicked the gravel. "So what can you tell us about the car?"

"This car's a one-owner," he patted the fender. "Lady lives in town. She works at the Safeway, so it doesn't have lot of miles on it for 2003 model. The tires are pretty new. I relined the brakes before it landed on the lot.

"And the radio works." Connie added.

He lifted the hood. "I tuned it up, as well. I can give her a six month's warrantee on parts and labor."

"Could we take her for a spin?" I tapped the fender.

"Sure."

"Why don't you go Zack? I drove it the other day. I better

stay with Katy."

As I drove out of the lot onto 101, I noticed the car had a little spunk. There didn't seem to be any untoward noises. The brakes worked. I tended to trust businesses in our town, especially ones that have been around for a while. If they try to cheat you, their business wouldn't last long. Word of mouth is not only good advertising but also a good deterrent for bad business practices.

Katy found a chair in the small dark office and I listened while Axel explained the deal to Connie with me peering over her shoulder to check the paper work as she signed everything.

They stood and shook hands on the deal. Axel dangled the keys in front of Connie. Sporting a huge grin, she took charge of them sliding the official paperwork in her oversized purse. For the first time since she'd been here in Florence I witnessed a smile that wouldn't quit.

As we walked out, Connie reached up and kissed me on the cheek.

"Thanks, Zack."

I smiled. "I'll help you with the car seat." I turned to Katy. This is your car now, Katy."

"I don't know how to drive."

"What if Mom does the driving? What do you think?"

"Does the top go down?"

"Not unless we're in an accident." Connie slipped in behind the wheel.

"And that's not going to happen because your mommy is going to drive very carefully."

"Yes I am." She turned to me. "I'll meet you back at your house. I'm ready to scrub and wax."

"Up you go." I buckled Katy in.

I watched them drive off the lot before I got back in my Jeep.

Chapter 44

Splash

The sun beamed through the clouds as I drove up to my house. Connie and Katy were there waiting. I opened the garage, took out the bucket, two big sponges and a little one in case Katy wanted to help. Connie turned on the hose while I dumped some soap in the pail. She put her thumb over the hose. A pathetic spray shot out on both sides of her thumb.

I loosed Snuzz who obeyed my commands. Wagging his whole body, he didn't jump all over the girls. But the water, that was something else. He did a crazy dance chasing the squirt of water. Katy took the hose and spun it around her sending Snuzz into a spin trying to catch the water.

"I guess you'll need a nozzle." After I screwed on the nozzle, I picked up Connie's hand and examined it. "You have fairly small hands for a grown up girl. Put 'er there." I held up my hand up. She set hers against mine, demonstrating how her tiny hand measured up against mine.

She smiled up at me with her shy blue eyes and thick lashes, glancing away almost as soon as our eyes connected. "Thanks." Then she tied her sweatshirt in front of her waist, rolled up her jeans, picked up the hose aimed and blasted the side of the car.

The skinny little kid sister had turned into quite a woman. I picked up a sponge.

"And we won't need your help. We're earning our own way." She grabbed the sponge out of my hand.

"Mind if I watch then?"

"What? Think I don't know how to wash and wax a car?"

"Okay, okay." I walked over to the back porch, signaling Snuzz to come with me. We sat on the stairs, Snuzz with his rear on the bottom stair looking like the boss.

I said a silent, "thank you," to who ever created tight jeans as Connie bent to dunk her sponge in the pail. The low cut tee peeking through her sweatshirt looked pretty good too.

Katy picked up her sponge and swooshed along behind her mom doing a fair job scrubbing things she could reach. I took out my iPhone and shot a picture. Katy turned around, stuck her hand on her hip with the other one thrusting her sponge in the air. I snapped a couple more shots of them both acting like a TV ad for Jeep.

"A little to the left. Don't forget the bumper."

"Which one?" Connie turned, aimed the nozzle and hit me square in the face.

That set Snuzz in a frenzy chasing the water.

"Why you…" I charged over, grabbed the hose, turned it on her and caught her back as she tried to escape. She threw the sponge at me.

"Okay, okay. Truce." I escaped with Snuzz dripping wet. He shook himself off all over me. I threw him a few tennis balls while the girls finished up rinsing.

"You can let the Jeep drip dry for a minute. However it's getting cold so maybe we better change out of these wet clothes. I have some dry sweats you can wear." I turned to Katy. How about some cookies and milk?"

"I want cookies." Katy came running.

Living in Mom's house where I could count on a jar full of home made chocolate chip cookies was going to be hard to face when I moved out. I put Snuzz in the back yard. He shook himself off. "You can't go in all wet like that. Stay."

I opened the back door for Connie as Katy skipped ahead.

"Hi, Mom. You remember Jules' sister, Connie."

"Well sort of. You're all grown up from the last time I saw

you." Mom gave her hug. "And who is this?" She leaned down to Katy.

"I'm Katy. I'm four." She poked four fingers in the air.

"Let me get you one of my sweatshirts before we have cookies." Mom took her hand as they danced down the hall to Mom's room. When Katy came back she looked like a doll in Mom's pink sweatshirt that looked like more like a dress.

I smiled. "Hey, you're pink like a princess."

Katy whirled around.

"Well, Katy would you like a chocolate chip cookie?" Mom reached for the cookie jar on the top shelf.

"Yeah, cookie."

"Yes, please," Connie reminded Katy.

"Please. Sit down." Mom said, exaggerating the 'please' She gestured to the table where she set the table with the plates and napkins. "I'll get some glasses."

I took the milk out of the fridge and poured a glass for Katy.

"We're going to change out of these wet clothes. We'll be right back, Katy."

Katy already had a milk mustache and cookie crumbs decorating her face. She wouldn't miss us.

Connie accompanied me down the hallway to my room where I grabbed some sweats off the shelf and threw them to her. "There's a bathroom down the hall."

Back in the kitchen I joined Katy and Mom. We were giggling and dunking our cookies when Connie came in, her hair clipped and piled on top of her head. Her hairdo and long gorgeous neck reminded me. I had once gone to see Jules and Connie in their ballet recital when both little girls had their hair swept up like that and pranced around in their tutus. Both girls had a classic ballet grace with an appearance that remained so today.

When we had finished our snack, I went in the cupboard and got out the liquid wax, a couple of cloths with a new chamois.

Katy touched the chamois then cuddled it to her face.

"Poopsie Lu would like one of these."

"Well Poopsie Lu will have to wait. This is called a chamois. Mom needs it to wipe down the car before she waxes it," I said.

Connie got to work dragging the chamois gently across the hood removing any water still on the Jeep, while Katy and I played with Snuzz. I taught her some hand signals and Snuzz showed her all his tricks. Katy acted like someone tickled her when he actually did his tricks for her instead of me. There's something about a giggling little girl that brightens the world.

After Connie had spread the wax on the car, the pale blue film set up. I went over, pushed my finger across the door neatly printing Katy's name.

"Hey, that's my name!"

"Can you write it?"

"Sure." She held out her index finger then wiped off a typical four-year old's version of how she thought 'Katy' should be written. Surprisingly recognizable, I smiled at the string of letters.

"Great! Now here, wipe this over our writing."

She smeared some more wax across our graffiti.

As Connie worked her way around polishing the car, strands of her hair loosened from her updo and curled around her face. Her face glowed with satisfaction. When she stepped back around, she popped up. "Tadah! Your Jeep Mr. Zack Langston."

I snapped a photo of her almost in an almost identical pose to Katy's, hand on hip with one arm in the air.

I snapped another photo of the two of them.

"That paint job on my Wrangler looks almost as good as your new blue Escort. Thanks." I leaned toward Katy. "And a special thanks to you Katy." I picked her up and swung her around. "You really helped your mom."

"Well, I have to get going. I promised Jules I'd get some groceries. I try to make dinner for her when she gets home." Connie jumped up and hugged me. "Thank you, Zack." She kissed me a short though ever so nice kiss. As she pulled back, she bore her eyes straight into mine. “Really Zack. Thank you so much.”

“Hey, good luck on your new job. Bye, Katy.”

“Me too!” Her little arms sprung upward. I lifted her up for a hug and a kiss.

I waved as they walked backwards then turned toward their new Escort.

Life is good. I smiled. It’s good to be home.

I grabbed a beer on the way to my room. The glow from the day lasted all evening until I came out to the front room.

“I’m going to watch the game. You want to watch with me?” Mom said.

As soon as I sat Mom said. “I know you’ve been...well different since you’ve been back. I can’t know or understand what you’ve been through unless you talk to me.”

“I don’t want to talk about it!” I grabbed the remote and tuned in the game.

“I’m here in case you change your mind.”

“I know.” I focused forward clenching my fists.

I woke late that night in a cold sweat, heaving for breath, having just faced an exploding IED followed by a volley of pinging AK-47’s that sent me running. I grabbed my favorite sleep medication, a bottle of Jack Daniels.

Chapter 45

Port O' Call

I struggled, rolling around the rest of the night, fighting off images that came when I closed my eyes. The next morning I woke realizing I hadn't taken my meds for the last couple of days. Maybe I'd start again.

I skipped breakfast opting instead for a cold Coors. I avoided Mom's stare of disapproval, grabbed a second one and headed back to my room. I searched for a couple of old text books I had that might give me heads up for what I might include in the port story and how I could present it. I finished off the third beer and lounged the rest of the afternoon on my bed to finish the last of my research. The next thing I knew, I heard a rumble. I sat straight up, my heart thumping in my chest. It was dark. How long had I slept?

Mom knocked on my door. "Didn't you want to go to that meeting at the Port Office? It's almost 7 o'clock."

"Yeah…Thanks…Have you fed Snuzz already?"

"I did."

"What am I now some kind of Mama's boy? I have to get out of here soon," I mumbled to myself on the way to the shower. Letting the hot water beat on my head revived me. Like a slow drip, the anxiety built, knowing this story could make or break my new journalistic career or leave me picking up a few boring stories a week. The doc told me stress was a factor in bringing on my episodes. I took a couple of deep breaths then slugged down an antidepressant. I toyed with the idea they were attacks but wouldn't let myself believe there was any serious problem - just episodes.

After I brushed my teeth, I gargled with mouthwash. I zipped my tape recorder with my laptop in my case. After I headed out to the garage, I knelt beside Snuzz and scratched behind his ears. "See ya." I waved to Mom.

On the way I thought through some of the topics Ms. Bauer had told me they were scheduled to cover.

Once there I crunched into a spot in the gravel parking lot. I found my way into the small meeting room filled with rugged men who I assumed were fishermen awaiting some decisions on the ice machine that had been in the works for years. The commissioners and the city manager sat in the front sorting out papers.

When they began to speak, I snapped the 'on' button on my tape recorder. They started with a discussion on revamping the boat launch area, with me taking copious notes on my laptop. Next on the agenda the commissioner announced the building of a new facility near the campgrounds. The builder presented some plans for bringing in a prefab building. By the time they discussed the construction of an outside bulletin board that would be in place beside the new facility to inform campers of the town's activities, sweat beaded on my forehead. Dizziness set in. I coughed. My throat dried to a crisp. How could they be nitpicking when there were people dying, soldiers being blown up, children being slaughtered because they wanted to learn to read, families dying because they helped the Americans? I closed my eyes and almost screamed out when a vision of Martinez stepping on an IED, blowing his leg off, spread in front of me. I shuddered.

"Are you okay?" The guy next to me touched my arm.

I jerked it away. I pulled at my collar. "Yeah. Sure." I squirmed while the group discussed the proposed ice machine. I finally burst out of my seat running for the door. The cold air hit me in the face. After a couple of deep breaths helped bring me out of my anxiety, I stared up at the blue-black sky filled with stars, the same sky that stretched over my old base in Afghanistan. I wondered how some of our friends in the Afghan Security Forces were doing, Haseeb and his family?

I sat in the jeep for a while until I saw that the meeting had broken up. I spent the next hour writing up the story. When I had finished proofing it, I emailed it to the paper along with the photo I took. Two things I knew. I could write a damn good story and I could never do that again.

Chapter 46

A Long Siege

I sped out of the port parking lot scattering the gravel behind me. Down Bay Street I found a spot near the Beachcomber. A lively crowd filled the bar stools, some couples leaned over their beers, but mostly guys stood around talking to the guys at the bar. I noticed a kid I went to high school with. "Hey, Russ. How's it going?"

"Zack. Long time no see. Where you been?"

I paused for a moment. Afghanistan fomented in my mind, but I did not want to think about it anymore. I especially did not want to talk about where I had been for the past four years. "I've been around. You see that Ducks game the other night?"

"They're burning up the court lately."

We talked a lot about the Ducks when Russ remembered a couple of plays by Josh and I when we played college ball. "Play some pool?" I changed that subject so as not to open another wound that was too sore to discuss.

I could see he hadn't played much. After skunking him the first game, I gave him some chances as I let him win the second game.

We talked sports, shot a few more games of pool, kept the Jack Daniels still in business. The next thing I remembered, I woke up freezing cold with day breaking over the Siuslaw. I had made it to my Jeep but never took off. The scene blurred - a smudge of indistinct buildings, boats accompanied by the sound of screeching gulls.

Rubbing my eyes, I sat up, stretched the kinks out of back then rolled my head around until my neck cracked. I turned the key in the ignition and aimed the car up to Highway 101. The liquor store lured me into the parking lot where I dragged myself in, bought 3 bottles of Jack with a beef jerky stick, which I gnawed on until I got home.

Snuzz waited by the door. When I opened it, his tail beat against the wall as he greeted me. I ruffled his fur then stepped by him. He just reminded me of things I didn't want to think about.

Mom wasn't up yet so I secreted the bottles of Jack Daniels past her room and headed down to my own room.

"You stay, Snuzz." He lay down, set his nose on his paws, pointing to my door as I stepped inside. I closed the door behind me leaving my conscience outside brooding on his paws.

I stowed two of the bottles under my bed before I twisted open the cap the third. With the pillows plumped against the headboard, I slumped on my bed, and tilted the bottle up to drink straight from it. The postered walls, photographs and trophies spun around me until I passed out.

The next few days were a blur, in and out of my stupor, in and out of Afghan scenes of violence, bloody confrontations while bombs blasted friends to pieces. I woke occasionally, dizzy, disoriented and reached for another bottle. I vaguely remember Mom leaving some food outside my door. I remember yelling at her a couple of times, but not much else.

Suddenly, I woke to the sound of the phone ringing. The digital clock on my nightstand read, "2:09." It was dark outside or I wouldn't have known if it was day or night. Getting up, overcome with nausea, I headed for the bathroom just in time to spill my guts into the john.

With the banging on the door, I yelled. "What d'ya want? It's the middle of the night."

"Zack! Are you okay? Open up Zack!"

"What?" I stood glaring at the wreck of a human being reflected in the mirror. The cold water I splashed on my face felt good. I cupped my hands and slurped, washing my raspy throat.

The pounding on the door continued.
"Zack, open up! This is important!"

Chapter 47

A Rude Awakening

I staggered to the door. "Yeah."

Mom stood there, pale and obviously quite distressed. "Jules needs you. She's at the hospital?"

"She…uh…okay?" My tongue seemed to fight me when I tried to speak.

"It's not her. It's her sister. Can't you talk to her?"

"What…? What happened?"

"I'm not sure, but Connie had an accident on her way back from Yachats."

"Tell her…be there is 15 minutes." I turned on the shower and stripped down; taking the fastest shower I've had since the cold water ones in Afghanistan. I finished off with an iced cold rinse on purpose to bring me to. "Please God… Connie and Jules." I tripped trying to pull on my sweats. While I headed for the garage, realizing God and I hadn't spoken for months. I wondered, "Why would God listen to me now?"

"You shouldn't drive." Mom stood in the hallway as I headed out to my car. "Let me have your keys."

"I'm Okay!" I dove into the Jeep. "Honest. I'm okay." I adjusted myself behind the wheel.

"I promised Juliana that I'd take care of Katy, but I'm not driving with you. Give me the keys." She reached in and removed the keys from the ignition.

Too dizzy to object, I slid into her Chevy and slumped into the front seat.

The seven-minute ride seemed to take an hour. My head

pounded. My mind raced. What if Jules had called earlier? Was I still too drunk to react? I focused hard on the lane in front of me.

If I thought I was sober, I was wrong. I got out of the car reeling. The pavement seemed to rise and fall with every step.

I fought myself to the front door of the hospital. Jules waited in the lobby with Katy who was curled up on the one of the chairs the waiting room fast asleep.

"What's wrong with you?" She backed away. "You smell like a brewery."

I tried to put my arm around her.

She pushed me back outside. "Zack! You're still drunk. It's been days."

"No. Not me."

Just then my mom came up to us. "Angie, He's not driving, is he?" Jules turned to me. "I don't want to talk to you until you're sober." She pushed me aside. "Go sleep it off?"

"Geez, why so mad..."

Jules hugged Mom. "She's in a comma, Angie. If you could just watch Katy until tomorrow, maybe longer." She handed a Minnie Mouse bag to Mom. "Here are some things for Katy...and her car seat. I want to get back to the doctor to see if there's any news."

"Everything will be fine. Don't you worry! I'll phone tomorrow and see what's happening." Mom turned toward me. "Get in the car, Zack." She pointed.

I didn't argue when I was seeing double as I looked over and saw Mom talking to Jules.

"Can you at least carry this stuff?" Mom handed me the car seat and Katy's bag.

Mom picked up the sleeping child.

Though I managed to carry the car seat and Katy's bag, I wasn't much help getting Katy in the back seat or getting her buckled in. I stumbled to the front and flopped in the seat of Mom's car.

"Geez! What was tha' all...about?"

"Zack. Don't you recall? Juliana called you multiple times the past few days. You were rude, sloppy drunk and... unintelligible. When she came over, you yelled at her to get out. There was a catch in her voice as she sniffled, wiped her nose. She stared ahead. "I'm sorry, but I told her you were on a bender and that this isn't the first time." She hit the steering wheel. "And this last time you made sure I knew I wasn't needed around either."

I hunched down in the seat.

"I'm taking care of Katy and I can't let you behave this way while she's staying at our place. So you need you get straightened out and you better do it fast or you'll have to find somewhere else to stay." The muscles in the side of Mom's face twitched. "Zack, I mean this. You better consider talking to the pastor at church. You need help."

Chapter 48

Tomorrow is Another Day

I barely remembered Mom getting Katy to bed in the spare room, though not anything about how I staggered to my room and sacked out on my bed.

The next morning, I woke with the sound of little feet racing up and down the hallway. I sat up hanging my head into my hands as if I could stop the pounding pain. As my first act, I reached under my bed, fumbled around until I found another bottle of Jack. Empties strewn across the floor and on my desk testified to the extent of my consumption. "Two fingers of Jack," I mumbled as I lifted the nearly empty bottle to my lips.

"Uncle Zack! Uncle Zack, are you awake. The sun is up. Wake up."

"Leave Uncle Zack alone, Honey. He'll be out later. Come on with me," Mom said.

I extended the bottle out in front of me, stared for a long moment then caught myself as I reared back ready to heave the bottle across the room.

"I'll be out in a few minutes, Katy."

"Good. Poopsie Lu and I want to have a talk with you."

While I was under the shower, I had a small vision seemingly rolling out of the steam. It only lasted a minute. Josh stood there, his Duck's uniform scuffed and grass stained, leaning against a locker holding his helmet in his hand. "You're a team player, Zack. Did you forget?" As soon as he appeared he vaporized back into the steam.

Looking into the mirror the revelation hit me. I was trying to play it alone when there were others on my team. I was letting them down. I puffed the shaving cream on a week's worth of beard and scraped my face clean as though I could scrape away the agony of my realization. Could I, would I actually do anything about it?

All I remembered clearly from the hospital scene the night before was Mom's strained voice telling me I had mistreated Jules when she came over and that I would have to straighten out or I'd have to find another place to live.

I walked slowly to the edge of my bed and dropped to my knees. "Lord, help me get through this day." I had no idea if he was listening. I do know that when I rose, I felt lighter.

I consciously chose an ironed buttoned down shirt, found a clean pair of jeans in the drawer and pulled them on. Tying up my tennis shoe laces, I made ready to face Mom and a little angel who literally stopped the Jack from sending me on another lost day.

When I opened the door, Snuzz, laid there, his head on his paws. He didn't jump up as I might have expected, however his tail was wagging. Had I disappointed him too many times this week?

"Hi ya, Snuzz, Old Boy. I knelt. He rolled over. Me giving his tummy rub probably felt almost as good to me as it did to him.

What could I do today to make things different?

Chapter 49

Make Amends

An irresistible aroma emanated from the kitchen wafting down the hallway as I approached the kitchen. No mistaking it. Homemade bread was in the making. Katy and Mom scurried around in the kitchen, each in a flowered apron. Mom's loaner on Katy, so cute, rolled up, tied high just under her armpits like a long dress. Mom, hands mitted, slid a loaf of bread from the oven.

"Say, you're looking better," Mom glanced over at me before setting the loaf pan on the cooling rack.

"Uncle Zack!" Katy roared toward me, throwing her arms around my legs. You're up! Grammy and me, we made bread!"

I held my head. "Wow! Grammy? That really smells good. And thanks, I am feeling better." I gave Mom a kiss and patted Katy on the head.

"Well, she had to call me something." Mom eyed me with a narrow glance. "I don't have any grandkids you know."

"When can we eat it?" Katy plunked her hands on her hips.

"It's hard to cut when it's warm but it's oh, so good that way. Let's let it cool for a few minutes."

I got out the peanut butter, a jar of Mom's homemade strawberry jam then unwrapped a new cube of butter. I handed three dinner knives and napkins to Katy. "Here, put these by the plates, please." I poured Katy a glass of milk. Mom and I had our black coffee.

Katy clapped her hands together while she watched Mom

dump the loaf out onto a cutting board.

By the time we had the table set, Mom had used her bread knife to saw several thick slices of bread. We all sat down slathering our bread with butter. I'm a purist, fresh bread with slabs of butter.

"Can I have peanut butter?" Katy asked.

"Let it sit on the bread for a minute so it can melt," I said.

After Katy's awkward spread of warm peanut butter on her bread, she held it in both hands and took an alligator-sized bite. Still munching a mouthful, Katy announced, "This is the best bread I ever had."

I finished off my first piece and launched into a second slice with slabs of butter topped with peanut butter. "Mmm, you're right. This is the best bread!"

"It's all about finding joy in the small pleasures of life." Mom said eying me.

Snuzz looked up at me as if to say, "Yeah, yeah. Simple pleasures, smeasures. Where's mine?" I held out a strip of crust. "Good, huh?" I scratched his ears. "I missed you, Buddy," I said thinking that I had nearly forgotten something. Having Snuzz in my life was simply a pleasure that I had been neglecting.

"Hey, Mom, how's Connie doing this morning?"

"The same."

"I'm going over to the hospital. Think Jules'll talk to me?"

"Only one way to find out."

Chapter 50

Just in Time

Katy reached up holding a slice of bread for her mommy then fixed another one for Aunt Jules. "Mommy likes jam. Aunt Jules likes peanut butter. So don't get them mixed up. Could I go?" she asked for about the 20th time.

"Sorry." I patted her head. "Maybe next time."

I stood there with the two slices, one in each hand until Mom rescued me. She packaged up the bread and handed a small paper bag to me on the way out the back door.

"You got a phone call from Terrie Bauer at the paper. The message is on the machine."

"Maybe I'll listen to it when I come home." I put my hands in my pockets. "Mom, I thought about what you said yesterday."

"I can see that today you seem...well...better."

"Things are going to be different. I promise."

The antiseptic hospital smell accosted me as soon as I rounded the hall. At the room I found Jules parents sitting in the hallway, her father reading the Register Guard as her mom thumbed through a Good Housekeeping magazine. "Hello," I stopped in front of them.

Lowering his paper Jules father said. "Oh hello, Zack," then refocused on his paper. Her mom faced me with a meek smile and went back to reading.

In the room, Jules lay back slumped in a chair with a book

spread across her chest, her head tilted to the side, sleeping. The sun streaming through the window, settled around her setting the scene like a masterful painting.

Monitors, a breathing apparatus, traction, multiple tubes and bandages rendered Connie almost unrecognizable. The heart monitor seemed steady though not entirely regular.

When the nurse came in to check the vitals, Jules wakened.

"Zack." She glanced up. "Hey, I'm sorry about last night...I was just so upset..."

"Never be sorry for telling it like it is. I am going to... well let's say I'm working on it. Today is the first day of my transition." I turned toward Connie. "What's the story?"

"No one knows for sure what happened. Connie only woke for a few minutes. With her injuries, I could barely understand her when she spoke, but it sounded like someone followed her. The fog settled in thick last night after a hard rain. Going too fast on a slippery road, she missed a curve, and drove off a twenty-foot embankment." Jules looked down at her hands. "Rolled the car. Lucky at that time of night a couple saw the car screech before she rolled over the edge. They called 911. The man and his wife said they did see another car close on her tail and that car didn't stop."

"What's the doc say?"

"If she lives...see, she broke two cervical vertebrae besides multiple other bones, has a severe concussion...I just don't know. He says we'll have to wait to see if she's paralyzed. Most likely she is. It just doesn't look good."

Jules got up rounding the bed. She put her arms around my neck. She whispered as she buried her head in the crook of my neck. "I'm so glad you're here." She pulled away and grabbed the bars around Connie's bed. She focused on Connie. "I just don't know what I'd do if I lost you."

"They're doing all they can."

"Will you pray with me?" she asked.

I took her hand and we bowed our heads in silent prayer.

Jules sat back down. "What's in the bag?"

"Here's a treat." I handed her the bag full of Katy's bread. "Mom baked bread with Katy this morning. I bet you haven't eaten much."

She unwrapped one. "Mmm, good.

"I didn't have the heart to tell Katy that her mother wouldn't be able to eat her slice."

"It's so wonderful of your mother to take Katy. My mom said she wouldn't be able to. She doesn't know what to do with small children. Besides she wanted to be here." Jules stared through the window. I knew how painful it was for Jules that her parents were so distant. I guess you had to give them some credit. At least they were here.

"Hey, look." I took out my iPhone. I thumbed through until I found the photos I took of the car wash.

"These are so cute of Katy. And that's the happiest I've seen my sister in a long time. Maybe you and she..."

That's when the monitors went crazy. A buzzer went off. Connie's frail body convulsed. Nurses stormed the room. "You'll have to leave now."

"But is she going to be okay?"

I took Jules by the arm, pulling her back.

"You need to go now!" The nurses busied themselves as the doctor rushed in. I ushered Jules into the hallway, pulling against my lead.

"What is it?" Jules father asked.

"Connie's monitors went nuts and..." Jules covered her mouth with both hands, paced, leaving the explanation hanging in the air.

"She began having convulsions," I added thinking they should know what was happening. "There are lots of people in there. They'll take good care of her." I tried to wipe the furrow of worry from my face.

Chapter 51

The Waiting

I folded Jules in my arms. She nestled there for a long while before she broke away. She resumed her pacing in front of me, past her parents still sitting there, frozen with an incredulous look on their faces.

"God never gives us more than we can handle." I didn't know where that phrase came from, but Mom had said that to me when I lost Josh. It comforted me, gave me strength, and it was something that came to my mind this morning when I wrestled with the bottle of Jack, when I resisted my urge to bury myself in self-pity.

Just then a uniformed policeman walked down the hall toward us.

"Ma'am, I was hoping to talk with your sister."

"She can't... She's been in a coma. Now there's a...an emergency." She glanced at the closed door. "The doctor's in there."

"We've talked with the couple who phoned in the accident. It'll be a while before we can check the brakes on your sister's car. Right now it looks like the weather, the slick roads, combined with the curves..."

I gritted my teeth. "I'm having a talk with that Axel Richards about that car he sold her." My hands balled into fists.

"Let our mechanics find out about that before you jump to any conclusions, sir."

My one hand still clenched as tight as I felt at that moment, I ran my other hand through my hair. My regulation cut had grown.

"But did that couple tell you about the car that followed Connie?" Jules asked.

"There might be something more to this. We have a partial license plate, but with the visibility... the couple couldn't tell us the make of the car or even the color, except it was dark. You said she worked at Ona's restaurant?"

"That's where she was coming from. It was her first night on the job."

"Well, we are checking into this. We had them take a blood sample for a tox screen."

"A tox screen?" Jules raised her eyebrows.

"Yes. It's pretty standard. The results are not back yet." He handed a card to Jules. "Let me know if your sister is able to talk to us or if she let's you in on more details. That's it for now." The officer walked down the hall then glanced back over his shoulder. "Sorry about your sister." He continued until he disappeared around the corner.

Jules and I lined up, leaning our backs against the wall in silence staring at our shoes. Waiting.

I remembered the night, waiting for the outcome, waiting for news of Josh, the doctor's words then the devastation the doctor's pronouncement brought for all of us. This just couldn't be happening...not again.

Chapter 52

Altered By a Moment in Time

The minutes ticked by, though long as it may have seemed, it wasn't many minutes until the doctor, came out. He stood in front of us. His expression was blank. As he turned away for a moment before addressing Jules, I knew. "I'm so sorry Mrs. Cole. We tried everything we could." He touched her shoulder. "The odds were so against her. Devastating injuries..." He took a step toward Jules parents who stood uneasily. "...and my condolences to you and your wife."

"No. No. She can't be gone." Jules stood frozen, her face contorted in agony. She banged the wall with her fists.

I held her against me while her body shook with sobs and her fists quieted against my chest.

Jules parents just stared wide-eyed at us. When I noticed a tear escape sliding down her mother's cheek, I reached an arm around her shoulder too. Her father hugged us all. It was the first time I had ever seen an emotion emanating from either of Jules' parents.

"What about Katy? What am I going to tell her?" Jules stared at me in horror. "What about Katy?"

The nurse came out from the room facing us. With concern she touched Jules' shoulder. "Would you like a moment alone with her?"

Jules wiped her nose. "You go, Mom." Jules said hugging herself and pacing.

We watched her parents go in for a few minutes whispering

to their lost child while holding her hands. Jules' Mom leaned over and kissed Connie's bare cheek. As her parents stepped through the door her mom wiped her face.

While Jules said her goodbyes to Connie, I stood at the doorway not wanting to intrude. Jules drew her chair close to Connie's side and took her hand. I couldn't hear what she said, but the body language spelled anguish. I knew I couldn't watch as the scene tore at my gut, so I walked down the hallway, took out my phone and called Mom with the sad news. "Please don't let on to Katy until we get there."

Jules walked into the hallway, red-nosed and slump-shouldered. "Why? What reason could there be for this tragedy when she had so much to live for?"

I wanted to do something to ease the pain of such a moment, but what?

We stayed at the hospital and made arrangements for Connie to be picked up and taken to the mortuary. There would be no autopsy as there was no doubt as to cause of death, just doubt as to the cause of the accident. I hoped the police were on it, though not much comfort would come from a conclusion that someone forced her off the road.

We headed out to the parking lot. "Are you sure you don't want me to drive you?"

Jules looked at her car and then back at me.

"We can come back later for your car."

"Maybe that's a good idea."

The rain started as soon as we walked out to the parking lot, seemingly wrapping the car in a cocoon of sorrow. The silence of the somber ride to my house was deafening.

Chapter 53

Coming to Grips

Jules and I sat for a few minutes in the car at my house. "Let's go in." I walked to her side, opened the door and took her hand. Dashing through the rain, we splashed for the backdoor of the house.

"Do you want me to stay with you while you tell Katy?"

"She really loves you, Zack. Would you please?"

"I'll be right there with you."

Snuzz met us at the door, sensing our mood, he followed, tail tucked with ears drooping.

Katy and Mom had been playing a card game when we arrived in the kitchen. Katy saw us down the hall. She scampered toward us.

"Uncle Zack! Aunt Jules! Where's Mommy?" I picked her up, hoisted her over my head, ignoring the question as I set her down.

"Thank you for the DE-licious peanut butter bread. What a good cook you are." Jules said smoothing Katy's bangs across her face.

Not saying anything, Mom just laid the deck of cards down, rose, eyes connecting to Jules. She walked around to Jules and took her in her arms. They held each other for a long moment.

Mom reached for the cabinet, took out a cup and saucer, saying, "You need a nice cup of tea. Let me get you some Milk and sugar?"

"Okay."

Mom brewed some tea before we sat down at the table together. Jules wrapped her fingers around the cup warming her fingers.

"Wanna play Go Fish?" Katy said.

"Not now Sweetie. Why don't you go get Poopsie Lu and Wolf Boy? Jules sipped on her tea.

"Okey Dokey." I smiled at the 'Okey Dokey', the words my mom had been saying to me for years and now passed it on like a smile gets passed on. I watched Katy skip away down the hall.

"Do you think you girls should say here tonight?" Mom said.

"Maybe so. I'm taking tomorrow off school. So I could go over tomorrow and straighten up the room Connie..." Her voice cracked. "... and Katy were using. It might make it easier."

"You can stay here as long as you like. I know you'll have a lot to do to get things settled." Mom pushed a strand of graying hair out of her eyes and sipped her tea.

"I don't have anything straight in my mind, yet. But Maybe Katy could stay here until I get it all worked out."

"I don't have that much to do right now and would be happy to babysit while you're working."

Katy returned with Wolf Boy and Poopsie Lu tucked, one under each arm. While we talked, Katy played with her dolls.

"Come on, Katy. Let's go into your room. We can all have a serious talk." Jules patted Mom's arm. "Thanks."

Snuzz lagged behind us as we walked to the spare room that Mom had fixed for Katy to stay in. I leaned against the desk as Jules lit the bedside lamp creating a spotlight on the quilt-covered bed.

Katy climbed up on the bed, sat her two dolls on the pillow then patted the quilt beside her. Snuzz accepted the invitation. With a quick leap he was up beside Katy. "Snuzzy took a nap with me today." She patted his head.

"Well that's something Snuzz does well, Nap. Don't you, Boy?" I squeezed him under his chin and scratched his ears while Katy hugged him.

How did Snuzz always know when someone needed him?

I pulled the desk chair over for Jules. I sat on the other side of Katy. Jules sat down, took Katy's hands in hers and focused directly into Katy's eyes.

"Katy, Dear, Mommy..." she swallowed so hard I could almost feel it. "Mommy isn't coming home, Honey."

"Why?" A quizzical look covered Katy's face.

"Mommy had a bad car accident. She was hurt pretty bad and God didn't want your Mommy to be hurting so bad."

"Can the doctor fix her?"

"The doctor said she was hurt too much to fix her." Jules eyes were full to the brim.

"But I made some bread for her. That will make her feel better."

"I know, Katy, and we gave her the jam bread and she said it was so good." I lied. "But Mommy couldn't get better."

"Can I see her?"

Snuzz inched his way over and laid his head in Katy's lap.

"No, honey. Mommy's soul has gone to be with Jesus in heaven." Jules smoothed Katy's hair and kissed her hands.

"Will I ever see Mommy again?"

"Mommy is up in heaven. She's watching over you and taking care of you. Even though you can't see her, she'll always be in your heart, too. " Jules touched Katy's chest. "Right here."

Katy seemed so tiny and lost as she leaned over Snuzz, laying her head on his shoulders. She wrapped her arms around him.

"She's your guardian angel watching over you." As she sat up, I kissed her forehead.

In the car, Jules and I had discussed the idea of Katy going to the funeral and being able to say her last good byes to her Mommy. We thought we might discuss it with the pastor. I had always heard that funerals brought closure, a sad but necessary step in accepting death. This very important aspect Jules didn't want to mess up.

Would saying goodbye to her mother at the service be too much for this four-year old?

Chapter 54

Straightening it All Out

That night, Jules and I tucked Katy in bed.

"I want Mommy to read me a story."

"You remember when we told you that Mommy was in heaven?" Jules sat on the bed next to her.

"But she's coming back."

"No, Honey, she can't come back. Lie down now. Relax and I will read you a story."

"I want my Mommy!" Within seconds the child's chest was heaving, bawling so profusely that it was catching.

Jules gathered Katy up in her arms and rocked while I helplessly turned, walked away, wiping my eyes.

Jules and I realized it wouldn't be easy for a four-year old child to understand the concept, the finality of death. I just didn't know how hard being the purveyor of that kind of information could be.

The room finally fell silent after an nearly an hour. So I peeked in. Jules lay curled next to Katy holding her close. I went in, lifted the Cinderella book off the bed, pulled up the comforter and covered them both in their silent slumber.

Walking by the phone, anger rose like a storm. Why did Connie have to leave this beautiful child? I found Axel Richard's number in the phone book. I pushed the number in. I knew if I drove there, I might…It scared me to think what I might do if I saw him in person. "Axel Richards. This is Zachary Langston." My fist clenched around the phone. "Connie had an accident. She drove your car off a curve two nights ago…"

"I'm so sorry. Is she okay?"

"NO! She is not Okay! She's dead! And if I find out that her brakes failed or anything in that car caused the accident I'm coming over there and make you sorry you ever lived. " I slammed the phone down, walked in circles while running my hands through my hair. I sucked in a couple of deep breaths. If I had gone to see him, I probably would have killed him. I took several more breaths letting them escape through clenched teeth.

Standing there by the phone, I decided to listen to the messages. I pressed the button. Ms. Bauer's voice came through the speaker. "Your story was good. It will be in the Wednesday paper. The check is in the mail. Come by to see me for another assignment." The message had been left days before and I had already received the check. After I listened to the message, I went outside. I gathered some firewood from the side of the house, stacked some logs next to the fireplace and arranged several on the hearth, rolled some newspaper and lit the fire while Mom rocked in her rocker. I flopped heavily in the old leather chair across from her, my arms splayed out on the arms with my head back staring at the ceiling.

"I don't know, Mom. I can't write those inconsequential stories, sitting there listening to people argue about miniscule problems that don't make much difference to anyone." I scratched my chin. "It's not like there's much money involved. I could hardly buy you a dinner out with the proceeds of a story, let alone pay for the gas it takes to get me there."

"Is it because the pettiness compares so to the dire conditions you faced in Afghanistan?"

Nodding, I leaned forward, laid my elbows on my knees with my head bent down."

"Can we talk about it?"

I rubbed my thighs. How could I tell her that sitting there in that tight little room had sparked a full-blown anxiety attack that set me on a bender? "I can't, Mom, because...I tensed up, almost passed out in that room. I went straight to the Beachcomber trying to stop the vertigo with Jack Daniels. Unfortunately that sorta works for a while."

"But drinking is just another whole set of problems."

Purposefully, I stood and charged straight to the kitchen, Mom on my heels. Like a parade, Snuzz was right behind. I went to the fridge and took out the last two beers, popped the tops and then looked at Mom, her face a mask of horror.

"Please Zack, don't!"

"Don't what? Pour it down the sink?" I held them up, pouring and watching the golden stream gurgle down the drain. I leaned against the counter. "That's the first step."

"So what's the next step?"

"I will take my meds until I can get an appointment with the doc in Roseburg. Then I need a job." I sounded very determined, but I didn't go to my room where I had stashed more Jack. I just wanted to know it would be there if I needed it.

We went back to the front room contemplating for a few minutes.

"Let's talk about what you would like to do, something you'd be good at. What makes you happy?" Mom asked.

"I like helping people, but I'm not rich enough to take up philanthropy." Just then Snuzz walked up and laid down carefully kneading my feet with his paws. With Snuzz eying me, the idea began to crystalize. "I just need to know if I could make money doing it. Dog training, dog sitting, working for a vet, at least I should investigate." We watched an NCIS episode while my thoughts kept jogging to what I should do next.

"You're a good boy, Zack. I know you can get past this." She walked over and patted my cheek.

"Knock it off, Mom." I force a smile. "I'm hitting the sack." But I had to get out on my own before long. That was part of what's next, on my way to turning my passion into profits.

I knelt by my bedside. "Please Lord watch over Jules and Katy. Help me be there for them, Jesus. Amen."

Snuzz viewed me as if to say, "I'm here, Zack."

Sliding under the covers, I wondered, "Without a few slugs of Jack, would I be able to sleep? Stroking Snuzz, I finally fell off to sleep.

The nightmare returned. This time, though, almost the instant I started tossing and turning, Snuzz whined softly in my ear. I let out a small gasp and I woke immediately, though not trembling. Snuzz interrupted my dream before any life threatening imagery haunted me into a cold sweat or fighting an out-of-control heartbeat.

"Thanks, Snuzz." I rolled him over and gave him a vigorous rub down.

There was a small rap on the door. I padded over in my boxers and peeked around the edge of the door hoping it wasn't Katy.

"Are you okay, Zack?" Jules smoothed her hair out of her face.

"Go back to bed. I'm fine. Just a dream."

"You want to talk about it?"

"Snuzz is watching out for me. I'm okay. How are you doing?"

"It's funny, but having Katy is making it easier for me because she needs me to be strong. Night." She blew me a kiss.

Chapter 55

A New Direction

Having just gone through the procedures with Joshua's burial, at least Jules had an idea what she needed to do to take care of everything. I helped her as much as I could. In between times I shot off my ever so short resume to several businesses whose ads I had seen in the paper, with no positive responses.

Jules made an appointment with Pastor Perez at the Christian church. A slight man, youthful and handsome, yet slightly graying, he always put you at easy with a touch or a smile. He advised her that Katy should come to the funeral to say her final good buys. We prayed for His guidance to help Katy and Jules. While I was there he suggested that I make appointment at the VA. He gave me a number to call. I wasn't sure that would set me on a path in dealing with my problems. More pills?

"Hey," the pastor handed me his card. "Give me a call if I can help you out."

"I will."

Afghanistan found it's way into my dreams, not every night, but Snuzz seemed to sense my need. When a nightmare was beginning he woke me immediately. I still experienced anxiety attacks.

I tried to go down to Miller Park for pick up game of basketball, however the bounce of the ball against the backboard with that raspy jangling chain unnerved me. Recoiling at certain loud noises still plagued me.

The day of the funeral came. It would have made a very sad

movie with a small group of mourners watching Connie's casket lowered into the ground. Several of her high school friends sniffled while little Katy hugged Jules' leg and I wrapped my arm around Jules shoulder. Connie's stoic parents grasped their hands in front of themselves, her mother's eyes brimming. For Jules the combined sorrow following so shortly after Josh nearly overwhelmed her. Her breathing was labored, her nose and eyes looked like raw meat and the tears flowed down her face unimpeded, but she held herself together for Katy.

That night I walked the floor suffering acute anxiety and I reached for the Jack again. I just wanted to sleep. The next morning, I promised it wouldn't happen again. It didn't…for a while.

The court gave Jules temporary custody until the final papers were drawn up and they gave her a court date. The matter of finding Katy's father presented another problem. Jules wanted to adopt Katy, but that was impossible until the father signed away his rights.

Jules kept me busy helping her set up the room for Katy. We painted the room pink. I made a canopy frame for the bed. Katy helped me paint it, while Jules sewed a ruffled cover for it. In a matter of two days the spare room went from a study into an adorable little girl's room. Katy's excitement grew as she helped transform her very own room. The project put a lot of emphasis on recovery rather than mourning for all of us. The physical nature of it kept my demons at bay.

When Jules went back to work teaching, I helped Mom with Katy. I worked on designing a poster along with business cards for Langston's Canine Training and Pet Sitting Service. One day, I was driving around hanging some of my posters in different venues, when I cruised by the Ocean Dunes Veterinary Center. I veered into the parking lot. If I could get in with a vet, quite possibly I could get recommendations for dog training or pet sitting.

My dog was with me, so if I got an opportunity to speak with the vet, I could show some off some Snuzz 'tricks'. That's when I noticed it. A small sign in the window said, "Help Wanted."

Being late in the day, I lucked out. If I was willing to wait Doctor Boseman would see me.

Taking my seat in the waiting room, Snuzz sat at my feet with his sniffer going crazy. When the last Pomeranian came prancing out, she sauntered up to Snuzz, whose only acknowledgement was to bend his head down to sniff the ball of fur. She started yapping, but Snuzz just gave her a look like, "Take it easy, Girl." The owner pulled on the leash tugging the Pomeranian to check out at the counter.

"Good boy, Snuzz." I gave him a neck rub.

"Hello, young man, my tech says you are interested in the job," the Doctor said.

"I am, Sir." I stood.

"This way." He walked ahead of me toward his office. "What makes you think you would be good working with animals other than having a dog of your own?" He gestured for me to be seated.

I gestured Snuzz to be seated.

"Before I enlisted in the Marine Corps, while I attended the U of O, I took a dog training class. I used those skills to train my own dog. In basic training, I had some experience training military dogs."

I gestured and Snuzz sat up. Then with another gesture, Snuzz prayed. "This is Snuzz." I signaled. Snuzz offered his paw. I reached down and shook. "He's a rescue dog I brought from Afghanistan." I signaled Snuzz to sit quietly at my feet. "For his own safety, he had to be trained to be quiet, to do his business on command, to hide, to bark, to attack and to sniff for IED's, et cetera, although he can also do many more of the usual tricks." I signaled and he lay down. On another signal he rolled over. "He can do his 'tricks', for lack of a better word, with hand signals or vocal commands."

"I'm impressed. However, you appear to be highly over skilled for the job we have in mind."

"Which is?"

"Clean up detail. Exercise the animals. Feed, water the animals plus clean the cages, maintenance of the outside, cleaning up the fecal faux pas." He smiled. "And general all-around help where ever it's needed."

"Then I'm your man."

"I can only pay you nine dollars an hour."

"That's good for now."

"When could you start?"

"Tomorrow I have an appointment. What about Thursday?

Doctor Boseman stood and reached across his desk. We shook hands. "See you Thursday morning at eight."

I nodded. "To be honest, I am hoping that as you get to know me, you will be willing to give me your recommendation for dog training and animal sitting." I handed him one of my cards.

"We'll see how that goes."

Chapter 56

A Big Decision

Getting this job seemed a good fit and more like setting me off on the rest of my life. There was something settling about it and I wanted to share it with Jules and Katy. Snuzz aimed his head out the window into the wind while I aimed the jeep in the direction of their house.

Before getting out of the Jeep, I made a call. Then I jogged up their walkway with Snuzz at my heels. I knocked. There was no answer but I had seen Katy at the window as I knocked again. "Hey, Jules, it's me."

"Come in, Uncle Zack."

When I entered Jules was slumped on the couch. She wiped her red nose and pointed to the unopened package sitting on the coffee table.

"What is it?" I asked.

"See for yourself."

I picked up the package reading, "Laugh While You Learn About Childbirth." I rotated the package. "So why aren't you laughing?"

She let one side of her mouth curl.

"The Lamaze DVDs?"

"Connie and I planned to do these together. She promised to help me. I can't..."

"What?"

"I can't do these alone. I need...help."

"I can help?" Katy stood with her hands on her hips

"Well, you see now, you don't have to do them alone. Let's all do them together."

She squinted up at me. Her furrowed brow began to relax.

"Here," I said taking my pocketknife out of my jeans pocket. "Let me open it for you." I slit the binding tape, slid out the container with 4 DVDs each labeled with their number printed and a brief description of their contents. "Hmm... Intro: Laugh, Learn and Exercise, volume Number One," I read the label on the cover.

"Before we start the Juliana Cole Official Lamaze Class. Let me give you my bit of good news." I snapped my pretend suspenders. "I am officially starting my job at the Ocean Dunes Veterinary Clinic on Thursday morning. It's only a maintenance job, however, I think it will help jump-start my business.

"That's terrific."

I slid the number one DVD in the Blue Ray player slot and joined Jules and Katy on the couch.

We started laughing almost immediately. The instructor was not only informative but good as any stand up comedian you'd see.

"Wait!" Jules paused the DVD. She jumped up. "I think I'll take notes." She brought back pencils with a binder labeled Baby. She tore out a piece for Katy, gave her a pencil. I smiled when they both started scratching notes on the paper.

Katy held up her 'notes'. I flipped her thumbs up, surprised that some of her scratching contained letters.

Katy fell asleep on my lap while we finished watching the introductory tape. The presentation provided lots of information about what was happening to Jules's body and the baby and what she could expect in each month of her pregnancy.

"As much stuff as I've been reading, I am surprised this lady gave me a lot of new information," Jules smiled up at me. "Thanks, Zack."

"I'll pick up exercise balls after my appointment tomorrow. We could start the exercises then. I reached for the package. "There's a book in the box, too." I lifted it out and handed it to Jules.

After she opened the cover, she focused on reading. I knew she was hooked.

"I'll see you tomorrow afternoon?"

"Uh huh." She barely glanced up as I slipped out the front door.

Chapter 57

A New Day

That night the dreams returned. Just when the darkest part of my memories seemed poised on the horizon, when a group of Taliban closed in with heavy weaponry aimed directly at me, when the first crack of gunfire exploded, I sat up wiping the sweat from my face. I felt a gentle touch on my arm. Snuzz was pushing me with his paw. "Thanks, Boy." I fell back to sleep smoothing my hand across his soft fur.

Early the next morning I pulled on my sweats and laced up my running shoes. Getting back in shape needed to be another of my goals. Snuzz and I hit the beach for a long run. The gulls swooped, squawked, and circled overhead. I appreciated feeling my heart beating, sucking in the cool sea air, and seeing the gush of hot breath streaming out in the cold. The fresh sea air, the waves crashing against the shore, the sound of their roar drowned out the world. I made a mental note to do this more often.

I had an appointment with the psychiatrist in Roseburg at 11AM. So I wolfed down a bowl of cereal before showering. While the hot water ran on my head, I thought about what I would say to him. What could he do, if anything, to help me? If he were like the base Doctor, I would just get another bottle of pills. Popping the pills didn't seem like a permanent solution. I began to tense. I'd have to talk about my experiences. This always peaked my anxiety. After I already rubbed the wetness out of my hair and off my face, beads of perspiration reappeared on my forehead. Snuzz stood there licking the water from my leg as I toweled dry. Laughing at him eased my thoughts for a moment while I pulled on my Levis and a sweater.

"See Ya, Mom," I yelled as I closed the back door. I led Snuzz outside. The brush of cold wind cooled me down. Noticing his sad eyes, I wondered if I should just take Snuzz along. I'd feel more confident if I took Snuzz with me, but chances are they wouldn't allow a dog. I always hate leaving him in the car, so to appease him, I threw a few tennis balls and tussled him to the ground, before I took off for Roseburg.

The problem with driving the long winding Route 126 to the 5 Freeway into Roseburg was the lack of traffic and the beauty of the scenery. Daydreaming, I forgot my speed. Some repair work stopped me. After checking my watch, I banged the steering wheel. The tractor didn't help my anxiety as it leisurely pulled back and forth, in no hurry to scoop up his load of dirt. I checked my watch again. I would be late if I didn't stomp on it. As soon as the worker turned the stop sign to slow, I jetted ahead, whirling around the curves. The speed gave mc a rush as I passed a slow car and just tucked in ahead of him before a truck loomed over the rise. After screeching around another curve and realizing that I had nearly lost control of my Jeep, I slowed, but not soon enough.

Chapter 58

Facing the Music

As the red light flashed in my rear view mirror, I checked my speedometer. It was tapping 68. I pulled over as soon as I found a wide shoulder.

The officer exited his car. Swaggering while opening his ticket book, he approached my window. I rolled it down. "Know how fast you were going when you passed that car back there?"

"No sir,"

"Sixty-eight is too fast to take these curves, not to mention passing at about 75. I hope that truck driver coming at you didn't have a heart attack fishtailing like that after you barely made it back in your lane."

"Sorry Officer." I hadn't even thought about the truck driver's reaction.

"Your license."

I started to reach in my back pocket.

He put his hand on his pistol.

"Just getting my wallet, Sir." I fumbled around in my wallet and my service ID fell out in my lap.

"A Marine, eh? Iraq?"

"Afghanistan."

"My brother was a Marine. So I'm going to give you a break. I am not writing you up for reckless driving." He handed me the ticket for speeding. "But watch yourself. Damned shame to make it home and then kill yourself."

"Yes sir, Officer." The sudden awareness that that could be

exactly what I was trying to do made me shudder and my hands shook when I slipped my license back in my wallet.

By the time I pulled back onto the road, I knew I would barely make my appointment. Since I couldn't speed, I just gripped the wheel, gritted my teeth and drove toward my destination. When I hit the 5 Freeway I made up some time.

I walked through the door into the shabby VA building at exactly 11AM. Typical of a government operation the drabness did nothing to ease my growing depression and anxiety as I glanced around the room. Vets of all ages bearing all kinds of physical problems eyed me as I made my way to the check-in desk. The guy just ahead of me, swinging between two crutches made my guilt bubble to the surface. Two wheel chairs sat waiting to my right with a one-armed woman to my left. Who did I think I was? What right did I have to complain about my problems? After checking in, I was about to turn and leave when I was called.

"Zachary Langston." The woman ushered me in to another waiting room. I sat alone as I filled out the inevitable clipboard full of paper work.

When the door opened, I stood in front of a slight woman that I estimated to be maybe 45, wearing a beautiful smile across her wholesome freshly scrubbed face. "Hello, I'm Dr. Tyler Reeves."

I had expected Dr. Tyler Reeves to be a man. Thus my surprise took me to a new anxiety level. I hadn't talked about my experiences with many people, and never with a woman. I remembered the base doctor, a male, how he had minimized my symptoms assuring me that the meds would cure all, which I now knew could not provide me with the relief I needed. Could this little woman give me more?

"Dr. Reeves." I shook her hand. Following her into the office, I fidgeting with my sweater neck before sitting across the desk from her.

She set her half glasses on her nose as she perused my paper work. "May I call you Zack? Most people call me Doctor Ty."

"Sure. Uh...Doctor Ty." My eyes wandered around the room noting that she had tried to de-militarize the room with a few pieces of artwork and family pictures.

She gave me her background, which included the usual college degrees and residencies. "My Dad was in Vietnam. He spent several years in alcohol treatment centers before he came back to our family." She pointed to her family pictures. "He is why I decided to pursue this career. However I think my most significant experience was my tour of duty in Iraq. My brother is now stationed in Afghanistan." Their pictures were lined up on the book shelves with her various medical books and framed licenses.

We exchanged the usual information like where we were stationed, etc. Then she volunteered some of her service experiences. Before long I found myself spilling out some of the specifics of my anxiety attacks along with the military episodes that triggered the nightmares. She had a way of asking just the right questions to keep me talking. It was like sitting with my buddy, Santos.

"The two things we'll be working on is your sense of purpose and trust. I can tell that you have already taken advantage of one of the most effective ways of dealing with stress and that is your dog. Your love of animals and the direction you are steering you life will go a long way in helping you work through your stress. Don't hesitate to use Snuzz to help. He listens?" She lifted her eyebrows.

"Yeah." I checked my shoes.

"Caring for animals is an awesome healer."

"I almost brought him today. Didn't think you let him in."

"Actually, I'd like you to bring him some time. Many patients bring their help dogs." She folded her hands in front of her. "You appear to be in pretty good shape. What about exercise?"

"Snuzz and I run on the beach quite often. I do some of my training callisthenics."

"Good. The running is excellent exercise. Besides the beach scene contributes it's own psychological boost. Which brings me to another good way of warding off an eminent attack of anxiety or claustrophobia."

"I guess a shot of Jack Daniels is not what you had in mind."

She smirked. "I think you already figured out that wasn't giving you the relief you needed. It's the one thing you can't give in to. It's only temporary relief. There are several well respected AA groups in Florence." She leaned forward and handed me a brochure with some phone numbers and meeting addresses.

"Deep breathing is an anxiety reducer. I'll give you breathing exercises next time." She sat up touching her gold loop earring. "Relax. Take a deep breath…Let it our slowly. Close your eyes."

I leaned back in my chair.

"Picture a serene relaxing place, a memory of a wonderful time. It could be one of those places you thought about in Afghanistan and wish you could be…"

Her silence gave me a moment to focus in on a scene. "Describe where you are?"

"I'm out on Lake Woahink. Surrounded by the greenness of the forest as its reflection sways on the surface of water. The boat is gently rocking. I'm fishing with my dad. The fog is lifting and the lake is glassy smooth with gentle circles appearing when something touches the surface." I smiled. "The fish are biting." I was surprised that I remembered that far back and it felt good to remember something without the element of fear or sadness. I was also surprised that I was smiling and not feeling sad about my dad.

"Okay. You are very good at descriptions. Now you have some homework to do." She folded her hands in front of her on the desk. "Go home and make a list of places, experiences that give you peace, symbolize serenity or give you pleasure. When you're ready to go to sleep is a time when this kind of imagery will help. Every time you feel an attack of fear, anxiety coming on, or every time you wake from a nightmare, stop, take some deep breaths and force your mind to go to one of these places. Can you do that?"

"I can try."

"Sometimes soothing music helps to produce the atmosphere

for you to recall these pleasurable experiences. This you can do any time to rest your mind, to restore your psyche."

"I'm not so sure my music collection of rock and rap music fits that description."

"Try finding some of those free stations, like Pandora, on the Internet. There you can select the type of music that suits you best; new age or smooth jazz are some of my favorites."

"Keep your exercise going." She rose. Shaking hands again as she gave me a pat on my arm with her other hand. "Someone once said to me that I owed it to those left behind to live life to the fullest." She rose from her seat. "Don't forget your prescription when you stop by the desk and make your next appointment on your way out."

"Thanks Dr. Ty."

"Nice meeting you, Zack."

I gave her a quick salute, while thinking about going by Jules' place this afternoon for her Lamaze work out – exercise would be good for both of us.

Chapter 59

Life is an Exercise

Mom and Katy were watching Sesame Street when I got home. Katy clutched the framed picture of her mom against her chest while she stared at the TV.

When the show ended, I walked over to Katy and held my hand toward her. "Want to go out to play with Snuzz in the yard?"

"I'll hold your picture, Honey, " Mom said.

"Okay." She reached up for my hand.

"It's been kind of relapse day," Mom said as she took the picture from Katy's clutching hands.

Out in the yard. I couldn't believe how Katy remembered a lot of the commands I taught her. Pour Snuzz, I thought, doing one trick after another must annoy him, but he seemed to enjoy doing his tricks for her.

Finally Snuzz reminded us by bringing over his tennis ball and dropping it at my feet, "No more commands. How about throwing my ball?" He sat glancing down at the ball, then up, eyes darting from Katy to me. He wasn't picky, "Hey! Just one of you! Throw it!"

After we tossed, threw and hurled the ball, Snuzz returned, panting while he headed straight for his water bowl. Back inside, Katy gathered up her stuff, kissed Grammy, took my hand and said, "Let's go home, Uncle Zack."

I phoned the school and left Jules a message that I'd take Katy home so we could start our exercise program.

"I got two kiddy seats at a garage sale on Saturday. You want to keep one in your car?" Mom said.

It didn't take a lightening bolt to make me realize that I was becoming very domesticated. A kiddy seat permanently in my car – I have to think about that one. I went ahead and installed it for today after pushing aside the three exercise balls that I had blown up at the bike shop. The medium one had to sit up front.

We got back to Jules place just as she drove into her driveway. I got the medium sized ball out and threw it on the grass. Katy ran after it, sat on it, bouncing around. "This is fun!"

I grabbed Katy's stuff and met Jules at the door. "Let me open it for you," I offered, as Jules' arms were loaded with some papers to correct.

"I'll be right out. I have to change. The doctor told me that it's important to wear the right clothes, most especially the right shoes while I'm exercising. Katy's ready. She's got her sweats on."

She smiled with her hands on her hips. "I'm ready!"

"Katy and I will get set up. Huh Katy?" I took her hand. "Come on out to the car. We'll get the mats and balls."

I moved the coffee table out of the way, rolled out the mats, found the DVDs. I identified number two, "Breathing, warming up, beginning exercises" I turned on the TV and slid DVD into the slot. I brought in a pitcher of water with three glasses. The internet information stressed that expectant mothers should drink a cup of water for every 15 minutes of exercise.

"Here Katy." I handed her the toys with her jacket that she had at my house. "Better put these away in your room so we'll have plenty of room to do our exercises."

She scurried off. She came back in with her arms tucked behind her. Then she popped Poopsie Lu and Wolf Boy out in front of her. "They do exerses too."

"Sure, but it's pronounced ex-er-ciz-es or callisthenics."

"Calisnics?"

"Close enough." I patted her head.

When Jules came back, I handed her first cup of water.

“We’re all playing by the rules. Bottoms up.” Katy and I took a drink too. I pushed play watching the TV for the menu then selected exercises. We sucked in some air through our noses and breathed out through our mouths, reminding me of three round-mouthed fishes with air bubbles rising. First the breathing then music played the right tempo for us to walk around the room, then to march. I couldn’t help thinking this is just what Doctor Ty suggested for me - breathing and exercising. We added some overhead arm movements, stretching adding some twists, all accompanying the right breathing. The music made it fun as it picked up the pace for different activities. Katy laughed as she paraded around the room with a doll in each hand.

After some regular squats, squats leaning to one side and then the other, the push-ups came next. Katy and Jules did the girls’ version from their knees. I did my push-ups with the boys’ version, braced on my toes. Katy laughed and watched while I double - timed mine some times clapping in between, sometimes doing them with one arm.

“Oh you big strong Marine!” Jules joked. “Such a show off!” She was breathing hard when she sat back. I pushed pause on the DVD player to let Jules take a breather with a second drink. After I said bottoms up again, the next set had us in a push up stance, walking our hands back and forward with bottoms up. That started us giggling so we pushed the pause button while we rolled around in laughter on the floor.

Katy liked the ball exercises best. We lined up against the wall leaning our backs on the exercise balls. Up and down we rolled against the balls. We sat on them as we rolled in circles. Squeezing them together in front and in back of us, we leaned this way and that. We did leg lifts. “This is a lot more fun than the callisthenics we did on the base.” We finished up the last set when the DVD announced, “Time for the cool down.”

The music was the same as for the warm up so we paraded around doing the same exercise as when we began. I marched right out of the house and left the girls to correct Jules second grader's papers. Katy's face lit up because she got to put the cute stickers on after Jules corrected them.

A really good feeling settled over me as I drove home. Nothing could spoil this day.

Chapter 60

A Job to Do

That night I lay in bed, arms propped behind my head, closed my eyes to visualize the fun we had that afternoon doing our exercises. However, the thoughts of starting my new job at the Vet clinic kept invading my mind. Would the same thing happen as at my last job?

It seems like I just closed my eyes when the dream started. I stood at edge of the marketplace, the soft wind carrying the sands in soft swirls. Suddenly the cloud of dust opened, full of exploding IEDs - everywhere I looked. Coming at me, screaming, "Allah," the man reached for the wirers on his chest. When he raced forward, panic enveloped me. As I ran the screams became louder and louder. I woke with the gentle push on my arm. I turned when Jules, said, "You're okay, now." I sat up surveying the room for Jules, but it was Snuzz pawing me. "Thanks. Old Boy." Shakily I leaned over wrapping my arms around him. I remembered to breathe in deeply a few times and pictured us running on the beach. Covered in sweat, cold and shivering, I sat up. I remembered the bottle of Jack under my bed. I couldn't close my eyes for hours, thinking that maybe just a few sips would help me sleep. I resisted until dawn when I roused Snuzz for a run on the beach.

I was still shaky and nervous when I dragged myself to the Jeep. On my way to my job at the clinic, I realized I hadn't done my homework. Dr. Ty had asked me to list places to visualize and I hadn't done that so I started thinking of my run on the beach, how the clean fresh sea air combined with the ebb and flow on the ocean.

That eased my tension.

I drove up earlier than I needed to be so I sat in the Jeep. While I waited for Dr. Boseman, I took several deep breaths as I visualized rocking in a fishing boat on a glassy lake.

When he arrived, Dr. Boseman introduced me to his tech. The young woman skimmed her long red bangs away from a beautiful set of green eyes. "Nice to meet you, Zack. Let me show you around."

Things were looking up.

I got busy right away cleaning out some cages. Walking a few of the overnight guests, I discovered the unruly King Charles spaniel was a real handful. His owner was scheduled to pick him up in the afternoon. Buddy definitely needed a trainer. After I grabbed a quick Big Mac, I spent most of my lunch hour working with him until that little brown and white spotted dog would sit or walk along with me without pulling his neck out of joint. Bringing the dogs out to their owners was one of my jobs. When I brought Buddy out, his first tendency was to race toward the middle-aged owner. I had him walking out, tail on high speed but staying with me until I handed the leash to her. "Sit," I signaled. "Mrs. Dickson."

She accepted the leash with mouth and eyes opened wide. "How did you do that?"

Once she had the leash the dog jumped up and down clawing at her legs.

"Buddy just needs to know who's boss." I signaled sit.

She ran her hand through her gray curly hair. "Yeah. He knows who's boss all right and it isn't me."

Dr. Boseman saw the whole scene as he sidled over. "Zack here…" he patted my shoulder, "is a darned good dog trainer." He turned toward me. "You have a card, Zack?"

I reached into my pocket. "Sure do." I handed her my business card. I showed her the signal for heeling and demonstrated. Then Buddy sat. "You can use voice commands or signals. I'm free Saturday afternoon, if you'd like to make an appointment."

"Saturday it is." She wrote out her address on a slip of paper. "One-thirty okay?"

"Perfect."

"Thank you, Mrs. Dickson. See you Saturday."

That's how my business started.

That night and the next day at work were like twins; a good day with the dogs and cats, another potential customer took my card. After a stellar callisthenics workout with Jules, Mom fixed a great meat loaf. When I went to bed that night, I felt good about my day so sleep came easily. It didn't last, however. Stalked by another nightmare, I woke, this time with a different ending.

Chapter 61

Facing Fear

Trying to visualize as I lay in bed, exhausted and waiting for my eyes to close, my eyelids felt like they were propped open with toothpicks. My visualization turned to the feel of Jack tingling in my throat and remembering that sleep might come with a little help. Just a few slugs wouldn't hurt.

I ignored Snuzz, my conscience, as he lowered his head and rolled his eyes up at me. I reached under the bed. My fingers toyed with the bottle and finally I drew it up, tipped it into my mouth downing the clear brown liquid hot against my throat and filling my being. Still close to dawn the nightmare returned and I woke up screaming.

Mom opened the door, took one glimpse at the empty lying next to the bed, stood for a moment, wiped her eyes then closed the door.

I lay there for a long while staring at the ceiling, my head pounding. Still a run on the beach might help. Snuzz and I took a short one between the early morning showers. Solitary on the beach, my thoughts turned toward Hayworth and other of my friends lost or injured. Why hadn't I done more? The, 'if-onlys' buzzed through my mind like a drill. Finally my splitting headache eased up as my mind focused on the ebb and flow of the tide as it bubbled into the shore.

My appointment with Pastor Perez was at 10 o'clock. Later I had my first dog training appointment with Mrs. Dickson in the afternoon. Could I pull it together? I didn't know but I headed for the shower, the great reviver.

I spent a moment apologizing to Snuzz and fed him his breakfast kibbles. Mom was another matter with her back turned toward me. She wasn't talking to me.

"Sorry, Mom." She turned looking over her shoulder. Her eyes said it all.

I fixed a dry toast and downed a cup of strong black coffee.

In the car I mentally reviewed the written stories I had sent over to Pastor Perez. It seemed easier to write them rather than to tell them. If he had an understanding of what went on during my tour of duty, he might have some insight to help me conquer my demons. Still I found myself gripping the wheel until my fingernails bit into my palms. I pressed the button changing my rock station to the classical music station, letting my mind wander into the Oregon woods. I relaxed a little. That is until I pulled into the parking space in front of the church.

I sat in the Jeep, frozen to my seat. I balled my fists and banged on the steering wheel. Why would God want to listen to me? Not when I was to blame… Not with all that death and destruction.

Chapter 62

Who Says It's a Wonderful Life?

At the Christian Church, I forced myself out of the car, approached the double doors, hands in my pockets, head down, kicking the gravel and clenching my teeth. Once inside the church, the secretary led me out to the pastor's office, past the soft music playing in the chapel, a brief interlude before I hurried in through the courtyard with the rain pelting down on me. Was the weather trying to tell me something?

Having been there with Jules didn't necessarily ease my tension. For that appointment I came there for Jules not me. After a handshake, I sat on the edge of my seat in front of his desk, glancing around at the bookshelves and over my shoulder, uneasy with the door behind me.

When a boom of thunder burst overhead, the windows rattled. I ducked and covered my head. Embarrassment burned in my cheeks.

"We all have fears, Zack. I usually take a few deep breaths when I'm feeling that way."

The pastor's kindly expression set the tone and I felt my tension ease a bit. I sucked in a long breath letting it stream out slowly. "My shrink said that might help. I just forget sometimes."

"Would you mind if we pray first?"

I shook my head and then bowed as he began to pray.

"Dear Heavenly Father, be with us today as we work together to help Zack step beyond the problems facing him. Ease his tension, Lord. Open his heart, in the name of him who taught us to pray. Our Father who art in Heaven, hallowed be thy name. Thy kingdom come. Thy will be done, on earth as it is in heaven. Give us this day, our daily bread, and forgive us our debts as we forgive our debtors. And lead us not into temptation, but deliver us from evil: for Thine is the kingdom and the power and the glory, forever. Amen."

I followed along repeating the Lord's Prayer with him. All through my childhood, every night I had said this prayer. I repeated it at various events where this well-known prayer was said, yet this was the first time the words actually seemed to apply to me, that as the words rolled out, my tension began to ease. "Thy will be done," I whispered under my breath.

"I have to confess, Pastor, I slipped backwards last night." I hung my head.

"And?"

"A week or so ago, I made a big gesture of dumping out some of my alcohol supply. I had stored my booze in a few other places, 'Just in case.' Last night was, 'Just in case.' The nightmares just wouldn't stop. I felt overwhelmed."

"You can't let this, the PTSD, define you." He opened a file where I could see that he had the stack of papers, the service related incidents that I had sent him earlier. He spread them out on the desk. Several places were underlined in a lime green highlighter.

"Have you ever seen the movie, 'It's a Wonderful Life'?"

"My mother's favorite Christmas movie."

"I understand that revisiting these incidents is painful…"

I leaned forward running both hands through my hair and then thrust backward, my hands behind my neck letting out a stream of air. I could feel my heart beat in my ears.

"…But follow me for just a moment. Imagine a world without you there. Firstly your mother would be childless and you know how she loves children."

I nodded. I remembered Mom's hysterectomy then thought of how she took to Katy. It occurred to me, without the pastor pointing it out, that Mom wouldn't even know Jules or Katy without me.

"There are several incidents in Afghanistan." He pointed at the papers.

Immediately I thought of Hayworth.

"Once you protected a mother and her child, diving over them as a shooting spree ensued."

"My friend...Hayworth. I could have saved him."

"Could you really? Perhaps he still would have died anyway. So would the woman and her son and most definitely you wouldn't be here."

He paused as I recalled the incident covering my face with my hands and then rubbing them on my jeans.

He turned the page. "Remember the girls' school? How many girls' lives did you save that day?"

"My team... they would have saved them."

"Would they have? You were there in that split second. You acted."

"I saw that scene differently. I saw the life I took."

"The one life for many." He flipped the page. "You and Mario Andretti."

I smirked.

"The bomb in that old car would have decimated your team without you jamming that Humvee in reverse."

I nodded.

"The biggest save was the IED plant you destroyed. You were the mission planner?"

I nodded.

"How many would have died if all of those individual IEDs and HMEs had been detonated? Not only that, you saved Santos and Haseeb's life. They were spotted and you took out the shooter so they made it to safety."

I could see where he was going yet I could still see every detail of that shooter's face as his life slipped away. "But if my friend Josh wouldn't have shoved me out of the way of the oncoming car, he could have leaped to safety." I felt the hot tears well in my eyes. "He'd still be here."

"Maybe not. God made a conscious decision to save you. He has a plan. He has a plan for you, but it's for you to decide. Will it be to drown yourself in booze? Will you let PTSD define you?"

I shook my head.

"You need to learn to trust. Then you need to find your purpose in life - the reason why you were saved."

My shoulders shook. I tried to hold back but this was the first time since Josh died that I let the sorrow over take me in heaving sobs.

Pastor Perez came around his desk and held me in his arms until I finished crying it all out. "Let's pray. Do you have something you want to say to God? Something you want to ask?"

This time we knelt together and bowed our heads. "Dear Lord…" I paused. What would I say? I swallowed hard. "I need your help, Lord. I don't think I can do this on my own and I'm in no shape to help Jules the way I have been. Lead me, I can't find my way or my purpose alone. Show me what you want me to do. Let me serve you. Help me fight my demons, and forgive me, Lord Jesus…Amen."

Was it a coincidence? As I stepped out into the parking lot, a golden rim of sunlight edged the deep purple clouds streaming streaks of sun, illuminating the parking lot. As I looked back toward the church, a rainbow arced across the sky then disappeared as I drove off.

Chapter 63

Finding My Way

I felt inspired as I stopped off at McDonald's for a Big Mac before taking off to my dog training session with Mrs. Dickson's King Charles spaniel, Buddy. The rain stopped long enough for some outside training. The session went well. After some reminders, Buddy demonstrated his ability to walk by Mrs. Dickson's side, to stop, and to sit. "Lot of practice this week, okay?"

"The only problem will be my husband. He indulges Buddy."

"Let's make our next appointment when he can be there."

"Next Saturday morning about 10 o'clock?"

"Ten o'clock. It is." We'll review this week's commands then Buddy will learn to come when he's called."

"I'd like to see that one."

"You will." I glanced around the room seeing the gnaw marks on the furniture legs. "We'll see what we can do about his chewing, too."

I went home to collect Snuzz for an afternoon run on the beach. How do you explain the difference? This morning's run was an angry run, feet pounding the packed wet sand. This afternoon's turned into a joyful run, including leaps, interrupted by some stick throwing and some cagey chase and tease games with my dog.

The day ended at Jules' house for exercises. I set the bag on the kitchen table before we started.

"What's in the bag?"

"It's for after." I came back into the living room and helped set up the room. "Poopsie Lu likes exercise. Wolf Boy does not."

"Are you sure?"

"Ruff, Ruff!" She wiggled Wolf Boy. "That's wolf talk for I wanna watch." She set him on the couch.

Jules and Katy were getting pretty good at the routines with the breathing exercises. Sometimes we took a laughing or giggling break.

Afterward, when we sat at the kitchen table, "Tadah!" I unleashed a bag of Oreo cookies from the paper bag. "I know we can't always do this because the baby needs a more healthful diet, but maybe this is exactly the accompaniment I need to tell you about my day. How about some milk?" I poured out three glasses.

Katy and I dunked our cookies in the milk. "Mmm, Oreos are good." Katy's mouth full of cookie rolled around with her words.

Jules reminded her, "Be polite. Don't talk with your mouth full."

I screwed open another cookie and licked out the middle. "My appointment to train the little cocker went really well."

Katy copied me with her Oreo.

"Oh you two are impossible." Jules dunked her cookie.

"What's important is I really wanted to tell you that my session with Pastor Perez was truly amazing."

"Oh?" Jules finished up her cookie then rolled the end of the package. "That's it for the cookies." Jules walked them over to a cupboard.

"Bummer." I scowled.

"Yeah, bummer." Katy said.

"Sit down for a minute. I want to tell you about my meeting with Pastor Perez." I waited until Jules sat opposite me. "We started with the Lord's Prayer." Pausing I rubbed my chin. "I experienced a remarkable understanding of the meaning the prayer. Instead of a rote bunch of words it became very personal, 'Thy will be done' part especially." I downed my milk, crumbs and all.

"Katy and I are saying the Lord's Prayer every night, huh Katy?"

"Yeah."

Jules tore off a couple of pieces of napkin. She wrote 'yes' on one and 'yeah' on another. "Here Katy." Jules handed Katy the paper that said, 'yeah'. "Your paper says, 'yeah.' Mine says 'yes'. Please give me your 'yeah'.

Katy didn't understand for a minute, so Jules traded papers. "Now your paper says 'yes'.

Katy's face looked quizzical as she examined her paper. "Yes?"

"I took your 'yeah' so you can't use it any more. I want you to remember to say 'yes' instead of 'yeah'. Can you do that for me?"

"Yeah."

"Did you mean 'yes'?

"Ooo-kaaay," she rolled her eyes. "Yes."

"Geez, now she thinks she's teenager." I smiled at Jules. How soon she had transitioned into a mom. Maybe that's how she was with her students.

"Wanna hear me say it?"

"Say what, Honey." Jules leaned close to Katy.

She put her little hands together. "Our Father whose art is in heaven… I forgot what comes next."

So we said the prayer all together.

"Pastor Perez is something though. Remember I told you that I sent him stories I wrote about some of my missions in Afghanistan?"

"Y-e-s," Jules exaggerated her 'yes' while getting right close to Katy's face.

"Anyway, he did a little run through like, 'It's a Wonderful Life.'"

"What do you mean?"

"Like what would have happened if I wasn't born. He made me see those missions in a different light. Not like the lives I took, but he reminded me about the lives we saved."

"Did you tell him about the time you saved me from burning

myself up in my princess outfit?"

I raised my eyebrows. "I really didn't think of it that way."

"What about the time you carried Johnny back from that hike where he broke his foot and couldn't walk. He would have been in real trouble if he had hiked alone with no one to go for help. You're my hero." She rolled her eyes at me.

"Come on now. I'm not a hero…"

"So what are those medals you had pinned all over your uniform?"

"Just in the right place at the right time."

"I bet Snuzz is glad you saved him!"

"I think it's Snuzz who saved me."

"Have you figured it out?"

"What?"

"A purpose."

"On my way home, I made an big decision." I paused.

Jules smiled up at me. "Well?"

"I'm going to switch allegiance from the Ducks to the Beavers?"

"Big decision? The Beaves? What are you talking about?"

"I am going to apply for the veterinary school of medicine at Oregon State. I went on the Internet to the University and sent for a packet of information and an application. I'm not too late for this fall if I get my papers and transcripts transferred there by next week."

"Wow. That is a big decision."

"I get a full ride with my GI status."

She shook her head. "I don't know what Katy and I will do without you."

"Well, that's months away."

That's when the knock at the door came.

Chapter 64

An Answer

Jules answered the door.

"I have some news about your sister's accident," the policeman removed his hat.

"Please come in. Sit down." He sat in the chair while Jules and I took the couch opposite him. I held her hand in mine. What would the news be? Lucky I came by.

"The tox screen came back." He turned away then focused his attention toward Jules.

"And?"

"She had been drinking."

Jules face reflected her great disappointment.

"How much?"

"She wasn't drunk, but with the storm and slick roads, it may have impaired her reflexes."

"And the person that followed her?"

"We don't know if that had any causal affect on the accident. We found the young lady who was following your sister's car."

Jules tensed while I realized I was clenching my teeth.

"She says she was following a bit close to your sister's car because the fog made it difficult to see the road ahead. She was depending on the car in front of her to help her read the curves."

"Why didn't she stop?" Jules voice was sounded strained and high pitched.

"She saw that thc other car veered over to the edge. She said that she had been to visit her boyfriend, but she told her mother that she was going to study with a friend. She is only 17 years old. She may not have exercised the best judgment, though she was sure the other people would be there to help."

"I see."

"The girl did make a 911 call a few minutes later but wasn't clear about what happened and she didn't leave her name. Guess she was afraid her mother would find out she wasn't where she was supposed to be."

"So in your estimation, she tried to make it right and bears no responsibility for the accident?" I said.

"That's right, Sir."

"What about the brakes? The steering?"

"They were functioning. They didn't play a part in the accident."

"You're sure about that?"

"Yes Sir."

"I guess I shouldn't have reamed Axel Richards out, like I did."

"I don't know if this is what you wanted to hear. But we are satisfied that we know as much as we are going to know about what happened that night."

"So this closes the investigation."

"Yes, Ma'am."

Chapter 65

Waiting for the Night

That night, I came in greeting Snuzz, who skidded straight at me down the hall when he saw me open the back door. "Down, Boy." I bent over. "Kisses, kisses." I pulled back. "Too juicy." I wrestled a bit with him. "Hey, what's that I smell?"

Mom stood by the stove stirring a pot of chili.

"It's just about ready. Hungry?" She dished up the bowls.

"Absolutely!"

I set the table.

"You look full of…well, way better than this morning."

"Sit down, Mom."

She sat across the table from me, concern on her face.

"It's going to be okay, Mom."

She smiled as I spooned the chopped onions over the beans before I heaped a mound of grated cheese on top. We discussed my day, my success with the dog training, my session with Pastor Perez and my decision of going back to school. When I finished my second bowl of chili, I stood. "Mom, I have something to do."

A quizzical expression settled on her face.

"Come and see. I strode into the back hallway down to my room with Mom and Snuzz parading behind me.

I took the last bottles of Jack in varying degrees of volume from under the bed, from my closet and from my duffle bag. "I wanted you to see where I stashed these. It'll take a while to trust that I mean this." I dumped my entire store of booze. We watched the golden poison drain down the bathroom sink.

The Ducks came on TV so we spent the rest of the evening cheering and eating popcorn, before I yawned and went off to bed.

The evening played out as an instant replay of a few weeks ago. I remembered my stash of booze was gone. I could do this. In bed, I grabbed my covers and rolled over. I hadn't forgotten my meds. Knowing that those meds very often didn't do much to ward off my nightmares, I laid there for a long time afraid to close my eyes. I said a prayer. The last thing I remember, I pushed Snuzz. "Move over Mutt!" I sprawled on my stomach and slept my first full night's sleep in a long time, a nightmare-free night.

Mom and I picked up Jules and Katy for church the next morning, in a burst of sunlight that matched my mood.

Chapter 66

Moving Forward with a Backward Step

It took several weeks to believe that the nightmares had ceased but they had not returned. I kept a couple of appointments with the psychiatrist and with Pastor Perez. However, my life slipped into a very comfortable routine. Up early I went for a run on the beach before going to my job at the Vet's office.

Being able to take Snuzz with me to work enabled me to take an apartment within walking distance to my job. I furnished it with some cast offs from Mom and Jules. Katy and Jules accompanied me to St. Vinnie's where I found some appliances. My bed was still a mattress on the floor, but Snuzz slept with me on far worse. Most of the artwork consisted of Katy's colorful crayon drawings I had taped up here and there on the bare walls of my apartment. The nights began with me still waiting for the nightmares that didn't come.

Jules health and attitude flourished while she grew rounder by the day. I continued my sequential photos of her tummy's progress. This time I tacked them to a corkboard in my kitchen. We continued the exercise sessions, though hers became milder with her second and third trimester, while I stepped mine up trying to keep in shape.

Strangely enough, many evenings often landed me at Jules' house at dinnertime. I scrutinized her doctor's recommendations for the ideal prenatal diet so I augmented that list with suggestions I found on the Internet. Therefore I often arrived with grocery bags full of vegetables, eggs for intelligence, and protein sources. Katy decided she liked eating her veggies, too.

I had received acceptance from Oregon State. That sent me

hunting for my old science books to study up to understand something more serious than James Patterson's mysteries. Dr. Boseman lent me some of his vet books. I wouldn't realize until I got there, exactly how intense the curriculum would turn out to be.

My list of clients increased, from my ad, from word of mouth, and from my association with Dr. Boseman's clinic. So I spent many evenings and weekends training. I kept appointments with some interesting pooches, or should I say I trained their owners to take command, all the while stashing some money away for when I wouldn't have time to work.

My friend Santos phoned one day in April. We'd shared a couple of calls, since he moved to Washington and I sensed, like me, that he had a difficult time letting go of the violent world we left behind in the military.

"Why don't you come down here, spend a couple of days with me?" I scrutinized my Spartan apartment. "Better bring a sleeping bag, if you've got one."

"It's a bright red one. Sure hope that won't clash with your décor. And I'd like that... I was hoping you could help me out with...uh with something I have put off too long."

"Sure. What is it?" I scratched my head.

"Let's talk about that when I get there."

Chapter 67

Some Things Are Tempting.

I answered the knock at the door. "Hey, Roberto. Roberto Santos." Still built like a bull, I noted. "How the heck are you?" Santos and I wrapped our arms around each other in a bear hug while we clapped each other on the back. "Come in to my humble abode." Snuzz wagged and kept pawing my leg, like, "Me too." Roberto dropped his duffle down next to his sleeping bag. He bent over to stroke Snuzz. What a mistake. Snuzz bowled him over like he was a paper lion. "Snuzz, why I think you remember me." Snuzz had Santos flat out on the floor kissing his face. Santos rolled him over giving Snuzz a good rub down. "He's fatter…" Santos leaned back. "And so are you! Better get you both on a diet." Santos headed for the fridge. "I brought some beer. You want some?"

I eyed the beer as he set the twelve-pack of Coors on the refrigerator shelf.

"A little early for me."

"Yeah, well I guess we can wait until later."

I pinched my chin in an imaginary rub of a beard. "Awesome facial hair."

He rubbed his beard. "Got tired of people asking about the scar."

"You doing okay? What are you doing with yourself?"

"You first. Gotta job?"

I reached in my pocket, got my wallet out where I kept my business cards and handed him one.

"The way you whipped Snuzz in shape, I'm not surprised."

I gestured to the imitation black leather couch where we flopped down.

"I work at a vet's clinic, that pays the bills but I'm keeping busy with dog training too. You? You staying at your parents' farm?"

"Nah. I gotta a place in town near a café where I wash dishes."

"Don't laugh. I'm now a Beaver fan."

"I like girls, too."

"No, I mean… I got accepted at Oregon State. I enrolled in the veterinarian school there."

"Hey. That's way cool." He watched Snuzz settle at his feet.

"I pictured you riding free on your horse, herding cows, or taking those aggie classes at Washington State. Cougars, wasn't that your team? You going to school in the fall?"

"Yeah, well… I haven't ridden since I got back. " He leaned forward with elbows on his knees. "Maybe next year I'll go back to school."

"So come clean. What's up?"

"I had to get away from home. My horse – Bandit." He held his head in his hands. "I had him since I was kid… My brother rode him to keep him in shape. He broke his leg in a riding accident while I toured Afghanistan. My brother only got a sprained arm, but they had to put Bandit down. "

"Sorry, man. I know how it feels. I lost my childhood dog while I was over there. It hurts not getting to say goodbye." Even after all this time I could feel the tears well.

We found ourselves staring at each other a bit red-nosed.

"Did you, I mean, are you, do you feel the same as when you joined?" Santos rubbed his hands.

"No one is the same, man. That stuff over there messes with your mind."

"I know you went to a shrink before you left…"

"I had some horrific nightmares, sweated out some anxiety

attacks, so yeah, I went into Roseburg VA facility a few times. The meds helped. Drinking didn't."

"It takes me a six pack at least to get to sleep."

"You want to know what really helped?"

"I'm not sure I want some shrink messin' with my head."

"You're Catholic aren't you?"

"You're not going to tell me to get religion, are you?"

"I'm just going to tell you what helped me. Okay?"

He nodded.

"I saw my Pastor. When we prayed the Lord's Prayer together, I suddenly saw that its words actually pertained to me."

"I haven't prayed in years."

"He's still up there, you know."

"Duh!" He shook his head and rolled his eyes at me.

"Anyway, the pastor made me realize how the missions we carried out over there, were different than my perceptions. I saw the death and destruction. He made me take another look at all the lives we saved."

"That's made a difference?"

"Remember the Girl's school?"

"I can still see that terrorist's face when I narrowed him in my sights then as our bullets pelted his body."

"And I can still see the little girl hugging you when you whisked her off the street just when that terrorist was about to take her down. That day, probably 20 or 30 girls and their teacher still live because we were there."

Santos hands shook.

"Let me try something. Take a deep breath. Close your eyes. Picture yourself off riding on the open range, your knees hugging your Bandit. The sun over head and wind in your face."

There was a simple smile on his face.

"Look anything's possible if you believe it is. My shrink had me make a list of serene, calming experiences that brought me some peace. She had me take a few deep breaths to visualize a soothing experience when I was stressed or when I couldn't sleep."

"And that helped?"

"I can't tell you what helped me, will help you, because it's my journey. You have to find your purpose, the reason why God wanted to save you. It wasn't to drink yourself to sleep or to wash dishes for ever."

I thought Santos was going to slug me. Instead he stood up and banged his fists against the wall. "I lost a couple of damned good jobs before I got this one."

Snuzz ducked at the pounding for a minute, then walked over nosing under Roberto's hand. In a few moments Santos reached down and stroked the dog's back. "I forgot how good Snuzz was at making you feel better."

"So maybe you need to get a dog?"

He tilted his head to the side. "Bandit was like that for me. I remember times when he would nudge me with that velvet nose of his until I paid attention to him.

"Hey, I got an idea. Let's go take a ride in my Jeep, top down. It's that kind of day." I walked Snuzz and signaled him to do his business before I put him back in the apartment. "Sorry Snuzz. See you later."

"A Wrangler, cool. Where're we going?"

"You'll see."

Chapter 68

Somewhere over the Horizon

We headed north past Fred Meyer's Market and came to the riding stables nestled against the hills. "If we can get horses, you're going to have to help me, because I've only ridden a couple times before."

"I'm not sure..."

"Sure you are." I hopped out. "Come on."

Santos got out hooked his thumbs in in belt loops and ambled over.

"There you go, Pardner."

We lucked out. They weren't booked solid for the day. Standing at the door of the barn, the youthful woman tucked in a plaid shirt to her old worn jeans. She led out Brutus, a spirited black horse for Santos and Jasmine, a chestnut brown one for me. Roberto smoozed his horse by stroking its neck and face. He whispered little somethings while he smoothed his hands across the horse's neck and backside.

Jasmine acted like Snuzz, nosing under my hand as I reached for her. "Just reminding me to give you a few pats. Huh? What a soft nose." Horses always made me a little fearful with their sheer size, but I was feeling a little easier after I patted her. "My Jasmine, what big eyes you have!"

Swinging up classy like a gymnast, Santos was into the saddle. With an, "oomph," I struggled up to hoist my leg over and find my balance on Jasmine's back.

After a few reminders of how to hold the reins with simple instructions on how to start and stop, we took off on a slow trot. We took the trail that led to the open stretch of the beach. Once there Brutus picked up the pace with Jasmine right behind while I gripped the horn, bouncing on her back. I think I preferred to run along the beach on my own two legs where I felt in control. Though there was that same wind-in-the-face freedom in a stellar setting of sun sparkling on the water, clouds sailing across the sky and the waves rolling in - invigorating to say the least.

We broke into a few brisk gallops splashing at the edge of the water, before it was time to head in. Santos rode tall, the hero in the movies, while I resembled one of the Three Stooges bobbing in the saddle, hanging on like I was on a rollercoaster ride.

Back at the stables, I swung myself off Jasmine almost collapsing when my feet hit the ground. "Well that was… uh stimulating." I rubbed my rear end. My legs felt wobbly.

"I don't think you could have persuaded me to do this if you had told me where we were going, but I'm glad you did."

"When we get back to the apartment, let me show you a website I found. It's a place in Washington you might want to try. It's a ranch where a psychologist had started a professional nine-week course. Veterans suffering from their injuries are matched with horses and trained to ride competitively in mountain trail riding." My legs quivered as we walked along. "I hope I can find the site again. At the time, the idea didn't appeal to me." I hooked my arm around his neck. "Hey, Bud. Whatever you do, I think it really helps to admit you can't do it alone then find some help."

We sauntered back to the car, side by side. "I don't think my legs are ever going to be the same again, Zack the bow-legged. Am I walking like a cowboy yet?"

"Yeah, you are. Riding takes a bit a getting used to. I'll have a few sore muscles too. But I haven't felt this good for a long time." He grinned.

"Say, what was that you wanted me to help you with?"

"Let's go back to your place first."

Chapter 69

Finding a Way

Back at my apartment, Roberto went over to his bag, took out a folded piece of paper, an envelope. He came over to the couch flopping down next to mc, cradling the envelope and staring at it. The paper had yellowed with a reddish brown smear that I recognized as blood.

"What is it?"

"Remember when Hayworth...when we were in the back of that Humvee trying to stop him from dying?" He slumped with the envelope shaking in his hands.

"Yeah. Pretty hard to forget."

"You handed this letter to me, Hayworth's letter to his mother. I tucked it into a pocket then transferred it into my things. Sometime after we got back, I wanted to take it to his mother. But when I got home, I couldn't find it. I can't tell you how guilty losing that letter's made me feel."

"It doesn't take much to intensify those feelings of guilt. Does it?"

"I was sick about it. I dreamed about it. Then just this week I found it." His hand flopped back into his lap. "After all this time. I don't know if it's right to go to her now, opening up this wound. Or maybe I am trying to rationalize losing it for all that time. Trying to figure out what to do. I could mail it."

"You have to take it to her."

"I know." He kept his eyes on me. "It didn't take me long to come to that realization. That's why I came here. Since we were together with him when he…" Santos choked up for a moment. "I hoped you'd go with me. Would you?" His forehead wrinkled into a frown.

The pain in my chest made me want to say, "No. He was your best friend." However, there was no way I'd want to go alone. So how could I let Santos go alone? "We'll go together."

"Thanks, Buddy."

We clasped hands while we bumped shoulders. "I have her number." He took out another scrap of paper. "She lives in Mapleton. I don't think it's that far from here."

"It's only about 20 miles up Highway 126. If we phoned her tonight maybe we could deliver it tomorrow. What do you think?"

"I'll call her now."

Fortunately she answered. Santos thought she sounded glad to hear some news of her son. He made an appointment to see her the next day.

"Can we take Snuzz? You know how good he is with people."

"Not a bad idea." I noticed my laptop on the box I used for a coffee table. "Let me see if I can find the website of that horse place I told you about. There it is."

"The website: Rainier Therapeutic Riding - in Yelm. Washington." He wrote down the information as I read it off. "Where is Yelm, anyway?"

"My parents place is outside of Yakima. Yelm is west of us, near Olympia, maybe 140 miles."

"You could drive by to check it on your way home."

"Maybe."

"Well, better put that info away in your wallet so you won't lose it." I slugged him in the shoulder.

"Okay, Okay."

"Would you like to meet Cole's wife?" I grabbed my cell. "I'll call her and…"

"I don't know…"

"You go to dinner with me. I go with you tomorrow."
"You're tough to get along with."
"Today turned out good so far, huh?"
"Yeah, it did."

Chapter 70

All that plus Dinner

I resumed my cell call, punching in the numbers. "Hey, Jules. My friend Roberto came down from Washington to visit me. If I pick up the steaks and whatever else we need, can we stay for dinner after we exercise?"

"Sure, maybe get some French bread too."

"Okay, See ya in a bit."

On the way over, I explained the situation with Jules and Katy.

Santos listened.

"I am working really hard on facing the guilt I feel because Josh isn't here when I am." For the second time I told someone about the vision I had where Josh spoke to me after his death. "So I am trying to accept the gift, and know that God has a plan." I laughed. "Wait'll you see this exercise program we do. I think there's enough room for us to do it all together."

"I don't know..."

"Trust me."

He rolled his eyes.

At Jules place I started moving stuff in the living room out of the way while Jules put the streaks in the fridge.

"Hey, where's Katy."

"Could you go in, see her, talk to her. She's having a bit of a downer."

I headed down the hall to Katy's room.

She lay on her tummy across the ruffled pink bedspread.

"What's the matter Katy girl?"

She rolled over snuggling Poopsie Lu to her. Her eyes and nose were red. "I can't remember it?"

"What can't you remember?"

"The song Mommy and I used to sing."

"Do you remember how it starts?"

"Jesus loves me…" Her face scrunched up. "That's all I know."

"Let's say a little prayer, okay?" I put my hands together and she copied me hugging Poopsie Lu almost in half.

"Dear Lord Jesus. Please ask Connie to teach us the song that Katy has almost forgotten." I took her hand. "Are you ready?"

I started in with the song. I hoped that I guessed right. "Jesus loves me this I know." Katy's little voice chimed in. "For the bible tells me so. Little ones to him belong. They are weak but he is strong. Yes, Jesus loves me. Yes, Jesus loves me. Yes, Jesus loves me. For the bible tells me so."

I couldn't help but think maybe adults should sing that song sometimes. "Shall we tell Mommy thank you?"

She clapped her hands together. "Thank you, Mommy."

"Are you ready to do our exercises?"

She slid off the bed and skipped through the doorway.

The exercises did exactly what I hoped they would do. We were all in joyous spirits while Roberto and I barbequed the steaks. The mood carried throughout dinner.

Katy had to sing her song again before she'd go to bed.

Driving up to my place, I remembered about the beer in the fridge. What would we do if Santos wants finish it off tonight? What would I do then?

Chapter 71

The Start of A Tough Day

As it turned out, we were laughing while reviewing the fun we had during the horseback ride, exercising with Jules and Katy, and at dinner. With such an easy transition, Santos, forgot about the beer. He fell asleep in his sleeping bag without touching a drop.

The problem was his waking. The next morning Snuzz pawed him awake, startling both of them. Santos leaped up, grunting into a fighting stance causing Snuzz to bark loud enough to raise the neighbors.

I wandered out rubbing my eyes. "Okay guys, truce."

Santos was shaking when Snuzz loped over to him. He nosed in with his usual nuzzling until Santos got down on the floor wrestling with him.

When Santos went over to the fridge and reached for a beer, I put my hand on his shoulder. "You managed last night without one. Let's go for a run on the beach first."

I didn't know what I'd do if he'd ignored me. However he shut the fridge door. "I don't know if I'm in good enough shape."

I elbowed into his midriff. "Yeah, you need to do something about that beer gut."

"Okay, Okay I'll go for a run. You got an extra pair of sweats, I just wore my jeans."

I threw a gray pair at him. "Let's go."

The fog was lifting as we parked by Driftwood Shores. Snuzz held his tennis ball in his mouth as he waited for me to open the door and let him out. He rushed out like an avalanche racing to the sand's edge, wagging his back end seeming to say, "What's keeping you?"

Santos started toward Snuzz running. "Race ya!"

He was at least 50 feet ahead, Snuzz at his side. I pulled on my stocking cap and dashed out after them.

I caught up just before the loose sand met the wet sand. I tackled Santos. Snuzz made the tackle complete with the three of us rolling around in the sand.

I reached for the yellow tennis ball and threw it. While Snuzz chased after the ball, we were able to get up off the sand. Bending over with our hands on our knees, sucking in cold gulps of air then trailing out our breath in the breeze, I said. "Hey, what do you say we start out in a slow jog? We can work into a comfortable pace." I brushed the sand off and he copied me. We took off down the hard sand, Snuzz trotting along trying to interest us in throwing the ball, which we did for a rest in between our jogs and sprints.

There's nothing as free as feeling like you own the beach. The only people on the sands were Santos and I, until we jogged on our way back. I waved to a couple holding hands as they walked along in front of the hotel.

All three of us were panting as we made our way back to the Jeep, but only Snuzz had his tongue hanging out.

"Shake yourself off." I signaled Snuzz. Sand flew everywhere. I poured him some water in his bowl before he hopped in the back seat. He sat poking his head through the front seats.

"Did we get close to wearing you out, Snuzz Boy?"

"That felt pretty good," Santos said collapsing into the front seat. "I think Snuzz could have done that all day."

"Yeah he's hard to wear out."

We stopped by MacDonald's on the way back - nothing like Sausage Mac Muffins and hot showers to finish off a run on the beach.

We took off for the Hayworth's house, with Snuzz facing through the window loving the wind blowing his ears back. The sun was inching its way through the clouds as the Jeep sailed along the glassy Siuslaw River on Route 126.

"Nice drive to Mapleton, huh?" Santos said.

Chapter 72

Closure

The Hayworth's home was one of the houses that stood on stilts along the Siuslaw River on the east side of the bridge in Mapleton.

As we drove up and stopped, I glanced over at Roberto, then muttered, "Dear Lord Jesus, help us out here."

We trudged though the yard, overgrown with native plants next to some huge ferns. Snuzz followed us down the stone path to the door. When I knocked, a few pieces of peeling blue paint flicked off. The door opened, the air filled with the scent of cookies. Both of his parents stood there for a moment.

"I brought my dog, Snuzz. I can leave him in the car if…"

"Well come on in here, Snuzz." She patted his head. "You boys, too." Hayworth's mother pulled Santos in and I followed. She hugged us both. "This is my husband. Mark,"

"Mark, I'm Zack Langston. This is Roberto Santos." Matthew's dad, a thin, wiry man, stuck out his arm and grabbed my hand then Roberto's.

"I'm Shirley…I am so glad you came. Come in. Sit down, please. Can I get you coffee, milk? Matthew always liked milk with his cookies."

"No thanks, but I will take a cookie." I gathered up a couple.

Flashing before my eyes, a picture of Matt's youthful freckled face munching one of those cookies his mom mailed him sent a sharp pain to my chest. I swallowed hard.

Santos and I sat down on the plaid tweed couch facing the

maple coffee table laid with a platter of peanut butter cookies. Snuzz sat dutifully at my feet. Sniffing, he sat unmoving yet staring at the cookies. Mark eased into in leather Lazy-Boy. I breathed in the pleasant scent of the cookies while I scanned the view of the placid river.

"These are great! Thanks." I wasn't sure how we'd begin. Having a mouthful of cookie put the onus on Roberto.

"Matt sure enjoyed those cookies you sent. He always shared them with us." Roberto examined his shaky hands then glanced from Mark to Shirley. "I am so sincerely sorry about...about waiting so long to get this letter to you. I misplaced it. Just found it last week." He slid his hand in his jacket, pulled out the envelope and handed it to her. "He had this letter with him that day."

"Would you? Uh... could you tell us what happened that day?" She clutched her son's purple heart in her hand.

Roberto tried to speak. He kept swallowing and fumbling with a few unintelligible syllables. "We uh..." he wiped his face.

"Would you like me to tell them?" I touched Roberto's arm.

He nodded.

"Your son is a hero. That day we were sent to a remote village where a sniper had been spotted on the second story. The Taliban held a family hostage. Bullets blasted all around us when we broke through the doorway. Matt saved my life, Cole's life and the lives of the woman and her son. He took out the Taliban that had me in his sights. I threw myself over the mother and child, while your son took out the rest of the Taliban, except the one..." I choked back, "...the one who shot your son."

Shirley rocked on the edge of her seat, dabbing at her nose and eyes. Snuzz drifted over and Shirley's hand gently began stroking Snuzz.

Roberto said, "I came in last. When we saw that Matt was injured we rushed him to the Humvee racing to get him back to the base. "His last word..." Roberto gulped, "...was, 'Mama.'" His shoulders shook and he gasped. "I'm so sorry. It was too late... He was my best friend...I miss him so much."

Shirley leaned over Roberto hugging and whispering in her tearful voice, "It's okay. It's okay." She smoothed his hair across his forehead and patted his back. "It's okay. God had his plan. He meant for my boy to be there - to save you all." Our eyes connected. "Bless you boys." She reached up for my hand and held it tight. "Go, Go and live your lives... Live without regret. Promise me."

I croaked out, "Promise."

She held the letter to her heart. "Thank you so very much. Your coming has meant a lot to us. You don't know."

That's when I noticed Matt's father, sitting with his face in his hands silently sobbing. Snuzz found his way there putting his head on Mark's lap. Slowly as he rubbed the dog's ears and shoulders, he regained his composure.

The ride back to Florence was a silent one, the bag of cookies sitting between us. Finally Santos spoke. "That was the hardest thing I have ever done in my life."

"Yeah,"

"Strangely though, I feel better. I was so afraid of this day. It's the first time since I came home that I faced that wretched day and really saw what happened. 'Why', has always been the question on my mind. Now I think I see why."

"Here Snuzz. Here's the cookie you deserve."

On my bed, after Santos was gone, I found a sketch he did of Snuzz and I on the beach.

Chapter 73

Moving Beyond

Besides our almost daily exercise routines, Katy, Jules and I journeyed on outings, went on picnics, took hikes along the rivers and into the woods. We introduced Katy to geo-cashing and enjoyed movies together. Before Jules got too round to do it, we brought Katy along and climbed to the tree house in Josh's back yard. Don and Kelly encouraged us to come over as often as we wanted.

I couldn't help but knowing that He walked by my side. I hadn't experienced one nightmare, or one claustrophobic anxiety attack. I was beginning to trust in the joy of living, and to find my purpose.

However, I still I couldn't believe it would be a long lasting reprieve. Had this immediate miraculous recovery ever happened to anyone else? I got my answer when Jules gave me a book for my birthday, Unbroken, a true story about a long distance runner named Louie Zamperini. He enlisted in WWII and became a bombardier. The Japanese riddled his plane over the Pacific. After the crash, he floundered in the open ocean for over 40 days sharing a raft with a couple of other guys. Their craft washed up on a Japanese island. Almost impossibly he survived another two years in merciless Japanese POW camps. He suffered starvation, constant torture with mind-altering brutalization. Louie came home a hero, but his treatment, his tortuous existence deeply branded his psyche. He lost himself in alcohol and mistreatment of those he loved. He revisited the anguish of torture over and over in his nightmares. Though he resisted, his wife persuaded him to attend a rally where Billy

Graham was preaching. At a second rally, Louie promised his service to God. From that day his nightmares were extinguished.

The reading of that book channeled my future planning. After finding out that Santos had taken my advice, enrolled in the equine program and had indeed returned to his church, I recognized that my influence helped him. I'd be able to do what I promised God. I believe that He directed my life to a profession that would lead to helping others. My skill with animals and my career as as veterinarian, would afford me the opportunity. I wanted to offer those in need of dealing with their traumas an alternative. I knew how much Snuzz helped me. I started a savings account with a plan to open a kennel where I could raise and train dogs as service dogs. As a veterinarian I would be able to gift the dogs to those in need and to share my journey with them.

I accompanied Jules to the doctor's appointments whenever I could. Everyone thought we were a couple, so we never tried to explain.

One night, at Jules' place, I carried the sleeping Katy to her room then returned to the living room. I plunked down next to Jules on the couch. Jules sat up, placed her hands on her plump belly. "He's active tonight!" She reached for my hand. "Here! Feel!"

"I felt it!" What an awesome feeling. "He kicked me!" I leaned down put my ear to the kick spot and whispered, "That a boy, you're already a place kicker!" I glanced up at Jules.

Our eyes met holding for a long moment. There was instant electricity between us. I felt my heart beating faster. I could barely breathe. It was like a slow motion moment drawing us into a gentle and passionate kiss. Arms around each other, we folded together. I had never felt that way about a kiss before, like it was the very first kiss in my life. I held her face close, kissed her cheeks, kissed her eyelids and kissed her lips. I couldn't seem to get enough. This time I knew or at least I thought she returned my affection. "I love you, you know?"

"I know..." She stood up suddenly, so quickly I didn't know what was happening. I sat there worrying. I leaned forward holding my head in my hands. What have I done now? I've ruined our relationship. She'll never be able to forgive me, to go back to just being my best friend. I felt sick. What should I do? Should I leave? Should I stay? I ran my hands through my hair as I stood. Could I pretend it never happened? I paced in circles. I blew into fists that had suddenly turned iced cold. I thought I'd explode until she returned with a paper in her hand.

"It's okay, It's okay, I think," Juliana sat down and I eased down next to her. She unfolded the piece of notebook paper. Immediately, I recognized Josh's scrawl across the paper.

"This came several days after you guys returned from Afghanistan. Just before..." She read in a wee small choked voice. "Jules, I'm looking at the Saint Christopher's medal you gave me. I keep it close to my heart and know that you are always with me in this far away place. There is a spirit in this medal. When this comes back to you, it will bring all the love and happiness with it. Love always, Josh"

Staring at the words, she sniffed. "Don't you remember, Zack? The medal came back in your hands." Juliana took my face in her hands and focused her brimming eyes on mine. "It was you. You brought the medal back to me, you bring me all the love and happiness."

He came two weeks early on July 26th. I was there at the birth of baby Joshua and saw him scream at his first breaths. "That's the Josh I know!" I held him in my arms.

So much has happened in this year. I started school in September. It is difficult to find time for everything, but we made exactly the right decision. Juliana and Katy moved with me to Corvallis where she started her new job teaching a first grade class that she loves, at the same school where Katy started kindergarten.

If you noticed that I started calling Jules, Juliana, I noticed it too. It seems that when she became my love, she became Juliana. When she is my best friend, she's Jules.

Kelly and Don were delighted with their new grandson. They also were very anxious to include Katy as their grandchild too, so it was a joyous celebration when Katy's father signed the papers. Juliana and I adopted Katy. I adopted Joshua Cole Langston, though he will know his father, and that he is the son of a very fine man.

This Christmas is our first together with baby Josh. I am fulfilling my promise to my buddy, to always take care of Baby Joshua and Juliana who has been my wife since last night at the Christmas Eve Service.

As I watch Katy and Juliana opening their gifts on the floor next to the tree, I hold Joshua in my arms, I pause, Snuzz pawing at the discarded wrapping paper and I glance heavenward, "Thank you, God, and thank you, Josh. This is my gift, my purpose. I will cherish it forever."

Joshua 1:9
...Be Strong and courageous. Do not be afraid; do not be discouraged; for the Lord your God will be with you wherever you go.

B I B L I O G R A P H Y and resources

Crisp, Terri: *No Buddy Left Behind: Bringing U.S. Troop's Dogs and Cats Safely Home From the Combat Zone*. Gilford, Connecticut: Lyons Press, 2011

Official site of the United States Marine Corps: www.marines.mil

Rainier Therapeutic Riding - www.rtriding.org
Eugene Oregon Register Guard, City Region, Sunday, November 11, 2012 (B1, B4)

Rivers of Recovery: www.riversofrecovery.org

Military Mental Health: www.militarymentalhealth.org

Marine Corps Community: www.marinecorpstimes.com

www.operationhomefront.net

Hillenbrand, Laura. *Unbroken: A World War II Story of Survival, Resilience, and Redemption*. New York, New York: The Random House Publishing Group, a division of Random House, Inc., 2010

Lamaze Information: www.babycenter.com

Baby Info: www.laughandlearn.com

Visual Mysteries abound in the workings of an author's mind, especially when the author is an artist.

Karen Nichols relocated to Oregon from Southern California where she was a teacher. She wrote and illustrated a number of children's books. Her artwork appears in books, in logos, and on book covers. Her fine art, sculptures, novels and poetry books are currently displayed in Backstreet Gallery in Florence Or.

She has written articles for the Siuslaw News and was the managing editor for Carapace Scrawlers Writer's Journal.

After taking a class, "Drawing on the Right Side of the Brain" she emerged with an adult book swirling through her mind. Thornton House , a mystery, is her first novel also set on the Oregon Coast. It is available at Amazon.com.

http://www.amazon.com/Thornton-House-Mysterious-transcends-deaths/dp/147014946X/ref=sr_1_8?s=books&ie=UTF8&qid=1344732440&sr=1-8&keywords=Thornton+HOuse

She lives in Oregon with her husband and Buddy, her King Charles Spaniel.

Made in the USA
Charleston, SC
28 February 2013